In the Image of
The Gardener

Arlene DeMar

Trilogy Christian Publishers

A Wholly Owned Subsidiary of Trinity Broadcasting Network

2442 Michelle Drive

Tustin, CA 92780

For information, address Trilogy Christian Publishing

Rights Department, 2442 Michelle Drive, Tustin, Ca 92780.

Trilogy Christian Publishing/ TBN and colophon are trademarks of Trinity Broadcasting Network.

For information about special discounts for bulk purchases, please contact Trilogy Christian Publishing.

Manufactured in the United States of America

10 9 8 7 6 5 4 3 2 1

Library of Congress Cataloging-in-Publication Data is available.

ISBN 979-8-89041-369-7

ISBN 979-8-89041-370-3 (ebook)

Dedicated with love & gratitude to:

Dad, *my hero*

Mom, *my "One Small Star"*

James...

Eddie & Cameo

~

C, L, W, B, P, & P

Thank you!

Contents

Preface

*"The LORD God planted a garden eastward in Eden,
and there He put the man whom He had formed."*
Genesis 2:8 (KJV)

Ad Majorem Dei Gloriam!

You hold in your hands the continuation of the delightful story, which began in my first novel, *The Coordinates of Time, Treasure, and Truth.* Likewise, the characters portrayed in this sequel are fictitious with the exception of numerous references made to historical figures such as Sts. Catherine of Siena, Thérèse of Lisieux, Monica, and Augustine—just to name a few. Like my first book, the Love that you will find threaded throughout the story is very real.

I wrote several reflections, which were thoughtfully placed within the chapters. I also prepared several retreats, and I hope that you will consider prayerfully participating alongside the characters.

Once again, I was able to include some of my artwork and poetry. All of the poetry was written by me, carefully selected from my lifetime's work or written specifically for this story, with two exceptions. The first is an excerpt from a beautiful, well-known poem by Robert Frost. The second is a stanza from a Christian hymn, which was made popular in the early twentieth century; it was placed at the conclusion of the chapter entitled, "A Glorious Easter Morning."

It has again been my pleasure to allow this story to germinate and come to life within my imagination and articulate it into the book you now hold—another true labor of love.

Continued blessings,

Arlene

Returning Snowbirds

Sarah and Jack Peterson own a vacation home down south, and, taking their cue from nature, they, like many other seniors, follow the birds who head south to outrun—or more accurately, outfly—the season's chill. Although they enjoy spending time there, each always experiences a sense of 'being home' upon returning to their primary residence. Their daughter, Amy, had just picked them up at the train station following four months of being apart, and each of their hearts seemed already full after the reunion. The Petersons are grateful to have had the opportunity to escape the harsh, sometimes bitter-cold northern winters, yet, they sensed a tad of relief as Amy pulled into the driveway.

It was late March, and the house was adorned with the many daffodils already in bloom in their garden. The flowers looked glorious in the bright morning sunlight, and both Sarah and Jack were warmed by the mere sight of them. It never ceases to amaze them how many different varieties there are. The various hues of yellows and even off-whites fascinate all those who are astute enough to pause, to take in the delightful display. Amy's older sister, Monica, had thoughtfully replaced the garden flag, which simply read, "Welcome Home, Mom & Dad."

Both Sarah and Jack knew from past experience that it would take a few days to unpack and feel settled. Once that task was behind them, Sarah had all intentions of going to visit her long-time friend, Gloria Morelli, who lived just up the street. She was eager to catch up with all that the four months had brought. She and Gloria had been friends since elementary school, and they were more like sisters than friends. Gloria was one of the nicest people Sarah had ever met, and Sarah knew deep in her heart that Gloria loved her dearly. Gloria repeatedly told Sarah that she was one of her treasures; this meant the world to her, especially since Sarah had no natural siblings of her own. The two women were sisters in Christ and each cherished one another in this way.

What Sarah didn't know yet however, is that sadly, while they were away, her dear friend, Gloria, had passed away just before Christmas. Although Amy had phoned her dad while they were down south to give him the sad news, she and Jack decided it would be best to tell Sarah once they returned home, as this would provide Sarah with the emotional support she would need. Although this was in Sarah's best interest, it was difficult for Jack to remain silent, yet he did this out of his love for her. It was also not feasible for the Petersons to make the journey back home since they had literally just arrived. It was too far away and far too expensive for them to have returned home. The difficult task of letting Sarah know lay before them on this otherwise pleasant spring morning.

Unpacking the Truth

Amy had told her father that she would stay awhile to help him break the sad news to her mother, and he was glad because he anticipated how difficult the conversation would be.

The three of them entered the house and found, just as in years past, that the refrigerator was full of fresh dairy products and that the pantry had been restocked with staple fruits and vegetables such as bananas and oranges. Also stocked were items such as carrots, onions, and garlic. Monica always took it upon herself to take care of this task for her parents when they returned home from any trip. This time, Monica had also stopped over just about an hour or so ago to brew a fresh pot of hot coffee. The familiar, robust aroma greeted them as they entered their sacred sanctuary. Alongside the plates and mugs, a cinnamon crumb cake sat on the kitchen table, waiting to be discovered. The table was also adorned by an exquisite bouquet of fresh flowers. The ribbon on the bouquet echoed the same sentiment as the garden flag, "Welcome Home."

Amy took her usual place at the table and assured her parents that they should take their time in settling in and that she was in no rush this morning. She was able to linger because it was Saturday, and she had already gotten a head start on her many errands. Sarah let her daughter know that she would just be a few minutes and that although she would unpack later this afternoon, there was one thing she needed to unpack now. Sarah and Jack had gone to a beautiful lighthouse on the coast and had picked up three souvenirs—one for Monica, one for Amy, and one for their younger brother, Keith.

Just as Amy pondered how thoughtful her parents are, a tear made its way down her cheek at the thought of informing her mother about Gloria's passing. Her tear is in no way surprising, as Amy has always been known by her family and close friends as one who had been given the 'gift of tears.' Her tear was the result of her consideration that at this moment, in her mother's mind, all was well, but she knew that shortly this would change after she and her father helped her unpack the truth of the way things had unfolded while they were away.

Jack made his way back to the kitchen first and, with only a look, conveyed to Amy both his gratitude for her willingness to be with him and his hesitation in saying what needed to be said. They had already previously agreed that they would not delay any further because if they did, then their having kept it from her would turn into deceit.

Sarah entered the kitchen and extended the souvenir to her daughter. As she did, she exclaimed, "Oh, it is so good to be home! Amy, you look so pretty this morning."

"Thanks Mom! How thoughtful." After removing the wrapping, she managed to say, "Oh, this is adorable!"

With that, Jack cleared his throat, and, after a bit more small-talk, he paved the way so that they could communicate the bittersweet news to Sarah. Once he said the actual words, Sarah turned to Amy as if seeking confirmation for what her husband was saying. Observing how difficult it was for her mother to process the news, Amy just nodded in agreement and, after a short while, found herself mustering through her continued tears, "Mom, I am so sorry for your loss."

"Thank you, Dear," was all Sarah could say as she processed the new reality in which she found herself. Her grief was as raw as it gets, and the lump in her throat seemed as if it could choke her. She and Gloria had been through so much together over many decades, and the thought of her not being here temporarily overwhelmed her. Jack, ever the gentleman, stood up and hugged his sweetheart as she began to weep.

"It'll be okay, Sarah. It'll be okay. We'll help you get through this."

"I know, Dear. Thank you." Initially, only one selfless question came to Sarah's mind, which was subsequently followed by yet another. "Amy, did she go peacefully?"

"Yes, Mom. From what I was told, she apparently was found sitting in her favorite chair in the den as if she had fallen asleep."

"By any chance, do you know if she was wearing her special hat?"

Amy's childhood friend, Cassandra, had given Amy all the fine details knowing that Sarah would want them, and from a place of absolute certainty, Amy quickly responded, "Yes, Mom. She was."

Unpacking this tiny piece of information seemed to ease some of Sarah's grief because she understood that Gloria had been in prayer at the time of her death. Although the connection to the hat made absolutely no sense to either Jack or Amy, it was a source of spiritual consolation for Sarah, whose simple response was: "It is so good to know that she was wearing her hat!"

Jack wondered if it would be a good thing for Sarah to take a nap and suggested that she might do so. She replied to the invitation, "Yes, Dear. That's a good idea. I'd like to take one in a little while, but if it's okay with you and Amy, can we just sit together for a while and have a piece of cake and a bit of coffee? I would like to celebrate the life of my friend, Gloria Candace Morelli."

Amazingly, Jack and Amy's responses were identical, "That's a great idea."

Hello, Goodbye, Hello Again

Amy stayed for quite a while as the Petersons shared stories of their time apart. It felt so good to be together again. The siblings agreed it would be best not to overwhelm Sarah, so Monica and Keith each planned to stop by at a later time to offer their support and condolences to their parents. The thoughtfulness behind their decisions always reflects the cohesion and love that the family shares.

For Sarah and Jack, it truly was good to be home, and for Amy, it was good to have her parents back. It was shortly before noon when she excused herself, knowing her husband and children would be waiting for her return. She had promised them hamburgers for lunch and needed to make a quick stop at the grocery store for a few items.

"I'll see you both during the week!" she called to them as she waved from the driveway, simultaneously blowing her mother a kiss.

"Yes, Dear. We look forward to it. Give those beautiful grandchildren of ours lots of hugs, and tell them we can't wait to see them!"

Amy's car was hardly up the street when Jack turned to his wife of forty-nine years and, embracing her, asked her if she was okay. "I suppose I'll have to be." Knowing her husband so well after all these years, she reassured him that he had done the right thing in waiting till they got home to tell her the sad news.

"Thanks, Sarah. It's hard to know what to do when things like this happen. All the kids agreed that if I told you while we were down south, you wouldn't have had the emotional support you would have needed."

"I'll speak to Deacon Josh in the morning, but for now, I would like to take that nap you mentioned earlier."

Sarah had hardly laid her head on the pillow when all the events of the last twenty-four hours came flooding back to her mind: the long, overnight journey home on the train, seeing her daughter, and learning of the death of her best friend. After thanking God for their safe journey, Sarah sighed while simultaneously taking a few deep breaths. With each inhalation and exhalation, a sense of peace slowly began to encroach on her feelings of sadness. It wasn't just *a* peace, it was *the* peace, "the peace of God, which passes all understanding."

Relaxing into the peaceful consolation, she drifted off to enter her dreams. At least there, she could still sit with Gloria and talk and laugh and reminisce—and so she did. Gloria was there, waiting for her in her imagination, and upon seeing her lifelong friend, Sarah asked her how she was doing. Gloria responded with questions of her own. "How are you, Sarah? I've missed you. How was your trip home?"

"*My* trip home?" Sarah exclaimed. "How was *yours?*"

At that, Gloria laughed, and through her laughter, she exclaimed, "It was wonderful!" Gloria's words were so reassuring and her laughter was so hearty and spontaneous that Sarah, despite her feelings of deep sadness, found herself laughing in reply. Sarah didn't quite know what she was laughing at, but what she did know was that it was good to be together again with Gloria, if only in her dreams.

Dreamwork

Sarah experienced many dreams over the course of her lifetime—prophetic dreams, inspirational dreams, and some even issued warnings. Because of the dream, she awoke from her nap with a sense of having just spent quality time with Gloria, and Sarah felt calm. Such phenomena happened on many occasions during Sarah's lifetime; she would think of something during the day, and although she initially didn't know why it was in the forefront of her thinking, it would occur to her that she had dreamed about it. This experience always fascinates Sarah who had also been blessed by God with the gift of dream interpretation. Sarah was surprised, intuitive as she is, that she had no premonition about Gloria's passing during all those months down south when she and Jack were enjoying the warmth of the sun.

In contemplating dreamwork, Sarah took a moment to reflect on how she had been so intrigued by dreams as a young woman that she often searched the Bible for those who also had dreams. Young Sarah acquainted herself with the likes of Daniel who saw the "writing on the wall," Joseph, the carpenter, whose dreams had provided instruction (i.e., taking Mary as his wife and traveling to Egypt with her and baby Jesus), and of course, probably the most well-known "dreamer," Joseph—son of Jacob, whose dreams led him on a path of unexpected twists and turns, causing him to travel down numerous and winding foreign roads.

This story, found in the Book of Genesis, was a heartbreaking one for young Sarah because it tells the account of intense sibling rivalry, which she could never comprehend because she had always longed for natural siblings of her own whom she could treasure. But ultimately, as Sarah matured, it became a story of God's faithfulness to Joseph as well as Joseph's faithfulness to God. For Sarah, it is a story of unwavering trust, redemption, and incredible forgiveness.

Sarah concluded early on that dreamwork is similar to poetry in that each requires some measure of interpretation. Through her studies, she learned to assess her dreams through a Biblical lens. Much like her friend Gloria, Sarah often expresses herself through poetry. For many decades, the two women had sat together, sharing their mutual gifts. Sarah would miss such experiences going forward.

The combination of the fresh dream, and seeing Gloria in it, reminded her of a poem Gloria had written as a young woman shortly after losing her dad. She knew Gloria had given her a copy of it and decided to search her journals to find the little poem hoping that it would comfort her now in this present, difficult moment. At her age, she had accumulated quite an assortment of journals; in looking through an earlier one, she found the object of her search. She discovered that the poem was accompanied by a gift of its own.

Oftentimes, when Sarah read Gloria's poems, she would place a sticky note on them sharing what stirred within her heart. The little yellow note on the page indicated the following: "This too brings tears to my eyes. Your expression is captured beautifully with both tenderness and longing." Sarah was deeply touched by her own reflection.

Sarah began to slowly, silently read the words her close friend had penned long ago, allowing her thoughts and feelings to wander where they may.

LET ME SEE HIM IN MY DREAMS

Star light, star bright, first star I have seen,

Wish I may, wish I might see my Daddy in my dreams.

Let him hug me, let him kiss me, let me know he's there.

Let him talk with me, for this is how he shows me that he cares.

Let him drive up with Mommy—coming from the store.

Let him be there when I get home—smiling at the door.

Let golf be on TV on a Sunday afternoon.

Let him be on the patio—smiling brighter than the moon.

Let him be teaching me to drive when I was seventeen.

Let him be there when I need him; on his shoulder let me lean.

Let him be in the living room, half sleeping in his chair.

When we ask if he's awake, let him sleepily say, "yea."

Let him be by the water, looking at the trains.

Let him see all the love my broken heart contains.

Let me hear, "Goodnight, Love" when I go off to sleep.

Let him know inside, his sweet memory I keep.

Let his shirt be blue, his jacket brown.

Please first star, don't let me down.

For in our hearts and minds is where he lives and breathes,

And that is why I ask you, let me see him in my dreams...

Closing the looseleaf binder, Sarah found herself hugging it because it seemed to connect her in some tangible way to those she had known and loved but had passed from this world. The poem was a beautiful tribute to Gloria's dad, Mr. Morelli. He was a fine man and remembering him brought Sarah comfort. Whispering a gentle, "thank you," she gingerly placed the journal back in the drawer.

Wiping her tears, she left her quiet space to join her husband in the living room. She knew he would be eager to sit with her and share his love; he would also help bear the burden of her loss.

Family, Friends, Flowers, and Food

Sarah and Jack were sitting together in the living room for only a short time when their son, Keith, arrived for a visit. Earlier in the day, he made a stop at his florist shop to finish a sympathy bouquet for his mother. He created a lovely arrangement with many of Sarah's favorite flowers. Keith is a highly-talented and sought-after florist in the region, and many people travel great distances to come to his store to purchase his floral arrangements. His love of flowers is not limited to floral arranging; it was Keith who had planted the display of daffodils in the front yard that had greeted his parents when they arrived home. His talent is not limited to flowers; it seems anything he touches is a beautiful work of art.

When he walked in, Sarah beheld her only son, her treasure, carrying the colorful piece of artwork in his hands. The joy she felt upon seeing him temporarily muted the ache in her heart. Somehow, he managed to simultaneously give her the flowers with one hand and hug her with the other. Addressing his mother, Keith explained, "Amy called to let me know that they told you earlier about Miss Gloria. I am so sorry, Mom."

Gloria was Keith's godmother, and although Keith Peterson is a grown man, well respected in all circles, he never stopped referring to Gloria as he did when he was a little boy. Calling Miss Gloria "Gloria" felt awkward and disrespectful to him.

His godmother often reminded Keith how grateful she was to count him among her many "Revolving Door of Friends."

"I know, Dear. Thank you. She was a good friend to me, and I am grateful she's with her Joshua now; I'm sure she's happy. She was your friend, too, Keith. How have you been?"

"I guess I'm okay. I miss going to her house and seeing her. I've known her my whole life, and it feels so strange that I can't pick up the phone or stop by to see her. She was always so kind and gentle. I made sure that the spray I made for her was especially beautiful."

"Oh, yes, Keith, describe it to me."

"I filled the spray with pink roses, snapdragons, lilies, and hydrangeas. It was absolutely gorgeous. I took pictures of it in the shop as soon as it was complete so I could show you. I *knew* you would want to see it."

"Did you bring the pictures, Keith?"

"Yes, Mom. Would you like to see them now?"

"Please."

Keith took out several pictures of the arrangement he had prepared for Gloria's wake. His mother gasped when she saw how beautiful the elaborate, pink spray was. Sarah was in no way surprised by its beauty, but rather, she was deeply moved by it. This is the effect that her son's work has on people. Whether Keith wears his florist hat or gardening one, each of his creations are given a great deal of care. He tends to each one as though it were his first project. Sarah and Jack understood the Divine source of his care, and it never ceases to move them deeply.

Since Monica had already placed a bouquet in the kitchen earlier, Sarah placed the one Keith brought on the coffee table in the living room. The sweet perfume emanating from the flowers was already lifting her spirits. Turning her attention off herself and on to the needs of her two favorite men, the souvenir they had brought back for Keith came to mind. As she excused herself to get it, she suggested they order a pizza in honor of Gloria because a fresh pizza pie had *always* been a big hit at the Morelli family home.

"Did someone say pizza?" Jack questioned jokingly. He hardly had the words out when he was already dialing the local Italian restaurant, whose phone number he knew by heart. "Hello? Bruno? It's me, Jack Peterson. How are you? Good, good…yes, yes, we got back this morning. I'd like to order the usual.…"

A Not-So-Early Wake Up

While Jack and Sarah were still at their vacation home, they had invited their entire family for a St. Patrick's Day dinner and asked them to reserve the first Sunday afternoon following their return home. Although the holiday itself had passed while Sarah and Jack were down south, they still wanted to celebrate once they were all together.

"All together" meant thirteen people for the Peterson clan. Jack and Sarah would be joined by Monica and her husband, Jeremy, and their son, Michael; Amy, her husband, Don, and their twins, Patrick and Patricia; and, last but not least, Keith, his wife, Barbara, and their two daughters, Rosalie and Lillian. When their pets are present, this total increases to sixteen. Their pets, or "fur babies" as Lily lovingly calls them, had each been named very deliberately. Since Monica's chocolate Lab was named Faith, Amy's family named their Welsh corgi "Hope," and Keith's family followed suit by naming their tabby cat "Charity." Charity was from the same litter as Katarina, Cassandra's family cat, and she is just as sweet. Actually, all three of the animals are sweet, and everyone is glad that Faith, Hope, and Charity get along, which allows them to gather together often without exclusion.

Although Sarah usually gets up at the crack of dawn, she was overly tired the next morning as a result of traveling, unpacking, and processing the news of Gloria's death. Still in her nightgown and slippers, she sleepily made her way toward the kitchen. Gratitude welled up in her as she remembered that Monica had stocked the refrigerator and pantry; this would allow her to prepare the homemade meal easily for tonight's gathering. Since it was a bit later in the day than usual, she would make a light brunch to hold her and her husband over until the family arrived later in the afternoon.

The Petersons returned home from Sunday Mass, and although they had hoped to run into Deacon Josh, they hadn't, so Sarah reassured Jack that she would give him a call during the week. Once home from church, Sarah quickly began making the preparations for the St. Patrick's Day party tonight. All of the vegetables had been chopped, and they, along with the corned beef, were already simmering in the slow cooker. Many wonderful aromas wafted through the home riding on the clean, fresh springtime breeze: the aromatic flavor of the coffee still lingered from the brunch, and the flowers' perfume continued to welcome them home. The corned beef spices emanating from the slow cooker, with hints of peppercorn, bay leaves, and coriander, was an Irishman's delight.

Amy likes to cook and bake, so she offered to bring her dad's favorite: Irish soda bread. Monica offered to bring wine, and as usual, Keith offered to make a festive floral arrangement for the dining room table. Keith's wife, Barbara, offered to make a pistachio cake because everyone loved it in years past and, of course, because it was green.

The grandchildren grew up on Irish music, and now that they were getting older, they offered to bring various devices on which they could play the Irish classics. The elders couldn't seem to keep up with such devices, but what they do understand is that although the devices may be new, the songs themselves seem ancient. Sarah often found that listening to Irish music—songs such as "Danny Boy" or "We'll Meet Again"—resonates so intensely in her soul that it seems to connect her to her ancestry in a deeply profound and indescribable way. Keith's personal favorites are "Red is the Rose" and "Lili Marlene" because his daughters are named Rose and Lily. Tonight, the Irish brogue of the tenors would fill their home—the mid-century white house with its black shutters on the quiet avenue leading up the hill.

Regardless of the reason, regardless of the season, any time the Peterson clan gets together, it is a time of celebration and joy because family means everything to them. The minutes were ticking by, bringing each of them closer to the time of the much-anticipated reunion.

Saint Monica

S arah and Jack's firstborn daughter, Monica, was named after her maternal grandmother. As the story goes, it is said that her grandmother was named after St. Monica, the mother of St. Augustine of Hippo, who prayed with dedication for her wayward son. Although Monica wasn't so sure she liked this association with her name, she was sure that she liked the name itself.

It is known that God uses all things for good, and Sarah found this to be true even in this seemingly small matter because hearing about St. Augustine and his mother at such an early age intrigued her daughter enough that she took it upon herself to begin studying the lives of the saints. Paying attention to his daughter's interest, Jack went to the local bookstore and purchased a child's version of *The Lives of the Saints*. Monica was around thirteen years old when she came to realize that she had been born on St. Monica's feast day, August 27. Monica's revelation was both music to her mother's ears and the impetus to Monica's understanding as to why her parents gave her the beautiful name.

Young Monica enjoyed reading the book her father had purchased for her and was eager to learn about a different saint each day. As Monica witnessed the lives of the saints from across the centuries, she could see that many were actually "sinners turned saints." She watched as one by one they traded their worldly pursuits for a deep devotion to God. Becoming acquainted with these men and women of the faith, who are honored and remembered for their having fully lived into the mystery of Christ, fascinated Monica.

As she followed the Sanctoral Calendar year after year, she became very interested in matters of the mind, as well as matters of the heart. She had a deep understanding that these individuals were *real* people who had *real* lives, with *real* trials and *real* accomplishments. She was intrigued by the many miracles associated with them. The most astonishing fact came when she learned that the bodies of many of the saints, such as St. Bernadette Soubirous and St. Catherine Labouré, were exhumed after death (for various reasons) yet still, to this day, have remained incorrupt!

As a young adult, Monica wrote a captivating poem as if through the lens of St. Monica for her son, Augustine, and this poem was the impetus for her wanting to help her fellow men and women with difficult issues they face in life—issues which might require another's help in processing. All the adults in her life encouraged her to pay attention to what was stirring in her heart because they recognized the insight the poem contained, and it was clear that her astute perception was well beyond her years:

> I had big, big dreams for my little boy.
>
> I was too young and too blind to see that the only dream that mattered was the one God had for you and that God's little dream was big enough.
>
> I'm sorry for the times I pushed too hard,
>
> Raised my voice, or spoke too soon.
>
> I'm sorry the world I birthed you in is not
>
> kinder, gentler, safer...

But there is way much more for which I am *not* sorry:

I'm glad that you are here.

I'm grateful you are mine, and

I know you are **deeply loved.**

God creates you day by day into the man He desires you to be.

Moment by moment, you fulfill God's little dream…

just by being you.

Thank you for being my beautiful son.

All my love, Mother

Birthed from her studies, compassion, and desires, Monica Peterson's attention was captured by the school of social work. She studied much and became a clinical social worker. Social Workers are not permitted to discuss their client's needs or situations, some of which are heartbreaking, so Monica is faithful to supervision and personal prayer. She maintains her license through continuing education. She is also a member of a local chapter of a Christian Therapist organization, which provides on-going support for the healthcare community. She, like her mother, also finds journaling helpful. She is well respected among her peers and, in addition to being considered a competent clinician, she is often applauded for her knowledge in the area of hagiography.

It seems that everyone who meets Monica loves Monica, and she is often relied upon for her wisdom. Jack and Sarah are very proud of their eldest daughter whom they had lovingly nicknamed "Little Saint Monica" a long time ago. On occasion, others in the family still refer to her in this way, and it always brings a smile to them all. To this day, All Saints' Day is a big celebration for Monica, Jeremy, and their son, Michael.

Amy, the Name Which Means "Beloved"

Each of the Peterson's children expresses their faith in God in their own unique way. Monica has come to know the saints so intimately that she refers to them as her "saint friends." Amy is more of a Bible scholar. As a young girl, she always enjoyed reading her Bible, studying it, and praying with it. Just as young Monica had been astounded to discover that she had been born on St. Monica's feast day, Amy was equally astounded to learn that her name was written throughout the Bible. Of course, she knew "Beloved" was written throughout the Scriptures, but one day she learned that her name, Amy, means "Beloved."

On the morning that she put two and two together, she ran around the house with the utmost delight telling everyone, "Look, look, my name is in the Bible!" all the while pointing to the word "Beloved" as she did. Each person she approached received the same explanation: "My name means 'Beloved,' and I am the Beloved of God." She took this revelation so deeply into her soul that she never, ever forgot it. Would it be that everyone, like young Amy, would hold this to be their truth: "I am the Beloved of God."

As a result of this experience, Amy developed into one of the most loving people Jack and Sarah have ever known, and, for that matter, this was pretty much the experience of most folk who knew her. Amy's fifth grade teacher recognized this love in Amy and suggested to her parents that they keep her sheltered for as long as they could. "Truly, her love is remarkable," her teacher had once said.

This sounded like a good idea in theory, but Jack and Sarah also wanted to parent appropriately. They couldn't lead their young daughter into believing she lived in Utopia, yet, they clearly understood the teacher's intent. They knew from their own experiences that life would educate Amy on situations that could, and most likely would, burst a sheltered bubble, and they also knew that her love of the Bible would certainly open her eyes to these situations as well. One cannot turn a blind eye to the stories it contains—Sarah had learned this early on with the story of Joseph, the "dreamer."

Meanwhile, Jack had come from a somewhat dysfunctional family, and he had determined long before he married Sarah that he would do his absolute best to raise his family in a functional environment where kindness and love were the order of the day. At the first sign of trouble amongst their children, he would gather the three of them together, even if one of them had not been involved with the incident at hand. Together, they would have what they lovingly called a "powwow."

The children who were involved with the offense had to sit alone in silence and think about what was happening and how their behaviors or attitudes may have contributed to the strife. Jack explained to them that it takes "two to tango" and that if they thought long and hard enough, they could see their contribution to the argument, rudeness, and/or dysfunction. The "innocent child," if there was one, had to observe; they could make constructive suggestions if they felt led, but this was not a requirement. Again, Jack took this very seriously, and they *had* to come up with some type of acknowledgement of their "fault" and offer an apology to the offended sibling(s).

This discipline was very difficult for the children at first.

Who wants to stop blaming the other? Who wants to admit that they were wrong? Who wants to seek another's forgiveness? And, finally, who then wants to apologize?

What Mr. and Mrs. Peterson found most interesting is that to their astonishment, the answer to all these questions, and more, was always, "Amy." She was always able to immediately admit her side of the wrong, and she was equally quick to forgive. Jack and Sarah took little credit for this uncanny ability Amy had to love, and gave all the glory to God for the grace she had been given. They always attributed it to that graced moment when she understood that her name means "Beloved."

As far as Jack and Sarah were concerned, this remarkable ability to love was truly astounding. They could see that most people were drawn to her because of it. In many ways, Sarah could see a resemblance in Amy that she saw in her best friend, Gloria Morelli. Sarah herself was an introvert off the page; Gloria was an extrovert, and so she discerned it best not to keep Amy in the bubble too long because it was probably God's will that she be out in the world—His world—making a difference. From this awareness, Sarah gently encouraged her younger daughter to join a local group for girls her age. Young Amy loved not only the idea, she loved all whom she met there, and they, in turn, loved her.

Keith—Third Child/ First Son

Jack and Sarah's diligent work to ensure brotherly/sisterly love amongst their three children yielded visible fruit, and this fruit was evident to all those who knew this close-knit family. Some said of the family that they were "as thick as thieves," and although neither Jack nor Sarah appreciated this particular description with its reference to "thievery," they understood this to be a compliment in its own backwards sort of way.

It is fairly common that younger siblings learn from, and emulate, their older brothers and sisters, and in this regard, Keith had wonderful role models in both Monica and Amy. It was his older sisters' interests that helped shape his own. Monica's love of the saints and Amy's love of the Bible made Keith thirsty to learn more of the things of God. The Bible passages that intrigued young Keith the most were the Creation accounts in the Book of Genesis; the saints that captured his attention were St. Catherine of Siena and St. Thérèse of Lisieux.

Recognizing Keith's interest in flowers and gardening early on, his family did much to encourage his love for them. Sarah would encourage her little boy to go to Miss Gloria's house up the hill to help her tend her garden. Keith learned a great deal during those early years he had spent with his godmother. Just as Jack had purchased a book on saints for Monica, he also purchased several gardening books for Keith. Keith became well versed on the subject of flowers and, like the flowers themselves, his knowledge grew and grew into a beautiful hobby and, ultimately, his livelihood.

Each time Monica read about a saint with an interest in flowers, she shared what she learned with her brother and Amy did likewise with her Bible studies. Monica still remembers the day she shared with Keith that St. Thérèse is a doctor of the church and that she is referred to as "the Little Flower." When Monica shared a passage from *The Dialogue* by St. Catherine of Siena, Keith came to understand God as the Divine Gardener tending to His "flowers," (His children) in His Garden. Of God, St. Catherine wrote the following: "You have come from me, the Supreme eternal gardener, and I have engrafted you on the vine by making myself one with you." Keith took the words of this fourteenth-century mystic to heart.

In studying the Book of Genesis, Keith came to understand that naming someone or something is a sacred task, which is as ancient as when time began. Per the Creation account in Genesis, it was God Himself who named the first man in the Garden of Eden; God chose the Hebrew name *Adamah*, translated Adam, which means "soil."

Through his contemplation, Keith likened Adam, the very first man, to a flower in an unusual, but appropriate, way. His insight was most likely birthed from St. Catherine's observation. Fascinated that a man came forth *from the earth*, his young mind immediately likened Adam to a flower. He saw Eve as a second flower. Each time Keith places a delicate ranunculus flower in a bouquet, his thoughts turn to Eve.

Many years ago, Keith had written a profound essay about Adam, which he entitled "In the Image of the Divine Gardener." He had given copies to his parents and sisters, and they were deeply moved by his insight. Years later, when the girls had gotten married, they shared it with their spouses after having obtained Keith's permission. All who read the essay were deeply affected by it.

Keith was recently looking for his copy of the essay but couldn't find it; it was very unusual for him to misplace any-thing, especially something he held so dear. He would ask his mother to see if she could find her copy.

Daughter- and Sons-In-Love

"Sons are a heritage from the Lord, children a reward from him," states Psalm 127:3, and in this regard, Jack and Sarah were blessed to have three grown children who were very much a part of their lives. As each married, first one, then the other, then the next, the number of their "children" doubled as far as they were concerned. Amy, their second daughter, married first. She and Don McDermott were wed on a beautiful spring morning, shortly after her twenty-fifth birthday.

Their eldest daughter, Monica, married the following year when she was twenty-eight years old. She married Jeremy, a Messianic Jewish man who brings another layer of richness to the Peterson family's faith. Through Jeremy's experiences, the Petersons have come to more deeply understand that the Old Testament is the New Testament concealed and that the New Testament is the Old Testament revealed. Jeremy and Keith hit it off on day one and have been the best of friends ever since. He and Keith enjoy sailing on the weekends on Jeremy's sailboat. Because of his relationships with Don and Jeremy, Keith now has something he had always desired—brothers.

Two years after Monica married, Keith posed two questions. The first was to his girlfriend, Barbara, "Will you marry me?" The second was addressed to Jeremy, "Will you be our best man?"

Both answered "Yes," with great joy. Keith's sisters and Don were also members of the wedding party. It was a warm celebration on an otherwise cold and wintry December day.

How blessed Jack and Sarah were by the three people who had joined their little tribe, not by birth, but through marriage. Sarah was quick to say that they were not their daughter- and sons-in-law, but rather their daughter- and sons-in-*love*.

Keith and Barbara were only married a few months when Amy announced that she was pregnant and, not only that, she and Don were expecting twins! This worked out well because she asked Keith and Barbara to be the godparents of one baby and Monica and Jeremy the other. It was about this time when Jeremy began sensing that Jesus, *Yeshua*, was the Messiah spoken of in the Old Testament, and after much prayer and discernment, he decided to join the Catholic faith. He was in the Rite of Christian Initiation of Adults program at Holy Family Church at the time, so he could assume this privileged role when the twins were baptized.

Our First Grandchildren, the Twins

Amy, Don, and their parents were proud to welcome Patrick Liam and Patricia Anne McDermott into the world. The twins were the first-born grandchildren on both sides of the family. During Amy's pregnancy, Sarah told everyone she met, "My daughter is going to have twins, and we are so blessed to have two grandbabies at once." On the day she had told Gloria the wonderful news, true to form, Gloria had a Scripture reference for her friend and did not hesitate to share it. "Children's children are the crown to the aged," and they truly are for Mr. and Mrs. Peterson as well as for Don's parents, Mr. and Mrs. McDermott.

Seventeen years have passed since the twins were born, and Patrick and Patricia are growing into fine young adults. Patrick's interests are focused mainly on baseball and golf. The one thing that everyone finds odd about Patrick is that, just like his dad, he doesn't have a favorite baseball team. Don doesn't root for any particular team because he enjoys the game more than the competition of it.

Camping is a favorite pastime for Don and his family. His daughter, Patricia, especially likes when the families go camping together. She particularly loves that these short vacations allow her to bond with her father, and she noticed that Uncle Jeremy seems to enjoy it almost as much as he enjoys sailing.

Patricia also finds interacting with other campers interesting; the people she has met are as diverse as the tents and RVs! She has found camping to be a bit of a subculture; it seems most campers they meet are friendly, relaxed, and helpful. After only a few camping trips, Patricia quickly concluded, *in this hectic world, who wouldn't like the relaxed atmosphere of the campgrounds?* Her favorite trip is the one they take by the lake. She loves the sense of adventure the campground offers, and the serenity by the lake reminds her of God's promise to "lead her beside still waters."

Michael

Monica's son, Michael, is fourteen years old, and although he is an only child, he feels as though he has siblings because of the close relationships he shares with his cousins. He has seven cousins in all, which include Patrick, Patricia, Rosalie, and Lily, as well as three cousins on his father's side of the family. Michael is an outgoing, likable fellow with many friends. He has close friendships with Gloria's younger grandson, Anthony, and their classmate, Philip.

Michael has learned much by watching his parents. He particularly admires his mother's ability to listen to others and how she is able to help them along their journey. His friend, Philip, who lost his own mother when he was a young boy, trusted Michael to help him cope with his loss. Philip wrote a poem about his pain and shared it with Michael, who felt privileged to have been given a copy of it. With Philip's permission, Michael shared it with Monica, who found it very insightful for such a young man:

Autumn Maple Tree

Sometimes I wish that I could be
just like the Autumn Maple Tree.
Many times, the wind has come around,
never once has it fallen down.
It is too high for you to reach;

a memory's held in every leaf.
When Autumn comes, the leaves must drop
and with them thoughts of these memories stop.
Memories of when the sun's rays burned,
Memories of the girl whose love was not returned.
Memories of the friends you must leave behind.
Memories of when the world seemed so unkind.
Into the wind these memories blow,
each succeeding harder to let go.
At last, the final leaf does fly—
but the Maple Tree does not cry;
Rather, it stands tall and high,
Keeping only what it has learned inside.
Sometimes I wish that I could be
just like the Autumn Maple Tree.
And not let pain live inside of me,
but learn what I can and set it free…

Through his friendship with Philip, Michael learned at a very young age how fortunate he is to have both his parents loving and guiding him. Philip and his dad are often invited to the Peterson holidays, and more often than not, their invitation is gladly accepted.

It is said that, "A dog is a man's best friend," and this is true in the case of Michael and Faith, the family's chocolate Lab who is very much attached to Michael. She follows him around wherever he goes, and Michael always takes good care of her. He feeds her, walks her, and is often seen playing with her throughout the day.

With names and saints being so important to everyone in the Peterson family, Michael is often quick to remind them that he "shares a name with St. Michael the Archangel." If the family heard it once, they heard it a thousand times, but no one ever gets tired of hearing it. They are all glad that this fact brings him such confidence and joy.

Our Garden: A Rose and a Lily

As previously noted, Keith has always been drawn to the Book of Genesis, particularly the Creation story highlighting God's naming of the first man, Adam, in the Garden of Eden. Adam, made in the Image of God, then turns and names living creatures: "Now the LORD God had formed out of the ground all the wild animals and all the birds in the sky. He brought them to the man to see what he would name them; and whatever the man called each living creature, that was its name. So the man gave names to all the livestock, the birds in the sky and the wild animals."

Keith believed that naming his children was a very sacred task, and he and Barbara chose wisely and prayerfully the names of each of their daughters. The first girl to arrive was named Rosalie Thérèse because to them, she was their rose, and on her birth announcement they wrote the words of Shakespeare. Since their baby girl was born on December 25th, the proud parents inserted one additional word: "A *Christmas* rose by any other name would smell as sweet."

Barbara enjoys reading about the life of St. Thérèse of Lisieux, a young girl, who lived out the charisms of the Carmelite Spirituality in the nineteenth century. Visible in the young saint's story are echoes of Salesian Spirituality as well, which Barbara also appreciates. St. Thérèse vowed that she would, "spend (her) heaven doing good on earth (and) will let fall a shower of roses." Rosalie's middle name is Thérèse, as a tribute to this lovely saint, and Barbara often prays for the intercession of St. Thérèse for her eldest daughter, Rose.

The last grandchild of Jack and Sarah was another beautiful little girl also born to Keith and Barbara. Lily was born on the first day of spring. Since she was the fifth grandchild of the Peterson family, and since five is the number which represents "grace," her parents considered naming her Grace, but instead decided to continue giving their children names of flowers. In this way, they could consider each of their children a beautiful flower growing in their family garden. With that, Keith and Barbara chose a beautiful name for Rose's younger sister. She was given the name Lillian so that they could call her Lily, Barbara's favorite flower.

Lily, too, had a personalized birth announcement, which had gorgeous artwork of lilies and the Scripture reference found in Matthew 6:28: "Consider the lilies of the field, how they grow." Truly, it was the Peterson's delight to look at Lily and watch her grow.

Aunt Amy created two copies of a beautiful plaque—one for each of Keith's daughters. On each one, she inscribed, in her best calligraphy, the following words:

"I am the rose of Sharon, and the lily of the valleys.

Like a lily among thorns,

So is my love among the daughters."

Song of Solomon 2:1–2

Birthdays and Other Celebrations

As the Peterson family grew in number, it was getting increasingly difficult for Jack and Sarah to keep track of birthdays and other significant dates, so Sarah decided to make a list for reference. On the list, she included their youngest daughter, Jessica, who hadn't made it to her fourth birthday.

Jack and Sarah were very sad to say goodbye to their fourth and youngest child, and although it was a long time ago that they had to say goodbye, sometimes it seems like it was only yesterday. At that time, Monica and Amy were old enough to understand to some extent what happened to baby Jessica, but Keith does not really remember his baby sister. Ironically, Gloria passed away on the same day that little Jessica had been born, December 11th. This connection made Sarah both sad and happy, but she couldn't seem to understand why.

Since the lives of the saints were very important to Monica, and the family as a whole, it was she who encouraged her mother to write down the particular saint to which each member of the family felt drawn. To this request, Sarah replied, "That is a lovely idea, Monica," and her research opened up conversations with each family member, which she otherwise might not have had.

Sarah found the conversations very intriguing as she

learned which saint each picked and why. Some were finding it difficult to name just one, so she assured them it was fine to pick more than one, and some did. Being so young, Rose and Lily were unable to name a saint, so their grandmother helped them choose. Since they both loved their cat, Charity, very much, she encouraged them to learn about St. Françis of Assisi, a humble friar who loved animals. The girls loved learning about St. Françis, and both happily chose him as their selection.

When Rose learned about his companion, St. Clare, she wanted to add her as well. When Lily heard that Rose added a second saint, she asked her grandmother if she could add St. Valentine because she loved all the red hearts and love, which February 14th represents. This encounter, which helped bridge the generational gap, could not have been more adorable.

Once the simple list was completed, Sarah went to the library and had copies made for Monica, Amy, and Keith. It was a loving gesture, and the kids were moved by both its simplicity and her thoughtfulness. Each displayed the list on their refrigerator for all to see and reference.

Birthdays

Jack	January 17
Sarah	March 21
Baby Jessica	December 11
Jeremy Cahn	August 11
Monica	August 27
Michael Aaron	January 7
Don McDermott	February 23
Amy	May 12
Patrick Liam	August 29
Patricia Anne	same
Keith Peterson	July 4
Barbara	April 30
Rosalie Thérèse	December 25
Lillian Grace	March 20

Anniversaries

Jack & Sarah	June 12th
Jeremy & Monica Cahn	October 6th
Donald & Amy McDermott	May 15th
Keith & Barbara Peterson	December 5th

Favorite Saint(s)

Jack	St. John of the Cross
Sarah	St. Françis de Sales
Jeremy Cahn	St. Paul
Monica	St. Monica & St. Aelred of Rievaulx
Michael	St. Michael the Archangel
Don McDermott	St. Ignatius of Loyola
Amy	St. Teresa of Avila & St. Thérèse of Lisieux
Patrick Liam	St. Patrick & Blessed Carlo Acutis
Patricia Anne	St. Anne, the mother of Mary
Keith Peterson	St. John & St. Catherine of Siena
Barbara	St. Jane de Chantal & St. Thérèse of Lisieux
Rosalie	St. Françis of Assisi & St. Clare
Lillian	St. Françis of Assisi & St. Valentine

Cenacle Spirituality and "The Extra Chair"

As the Peterson children matured and began marrying, Jack suggested that they upgrade their dining room table to accommodate the growing bunch. Jack took his role as patriarch and spiritual leader of the Peterson family to heart, and this was even evident in the ordinary task of replacing the dining room table.

Both Jack and Sarah spent a great deal of time at the local Cenacle Retreat House and were familiar with the charisms of the Society of Our Lady of the Cenacle. The name Cenacle, which means "retreat house," gets its etymology from the Latin, *Cenaculum*, which is the Upper Room where Jesus and his disciples had the Last Supper. One day, while reflecting on this, it occurred to Jack that he, too, wanted to embrace the practice that "all are welcome at the table."

Jack and Sarah went to several local furniture stores before finding a table they really liked. The model in the showroom only seated eight, but, much to their delight, the saleswoman informed them that they also had models that could seat either ten or twelve. Thankfully, after taking all the measurements, they could see that the table for twelve would definitely fit in their dining room and that the family would still have plenty of room to move around it.

Before donating the old dining room table, Jack had an idea, which was birthed from his contemplation of the Cenacle charism. He ran the idea by his wife. "What if we keep two of the chairs from the old table? The new owner will still have six. We can keep them on standby, so to speak. They would fit on either side of the hutch for extra company."

"I suppose that would be okay," was Sarah's hesitant response; she was confused as to why in the world he wanted to do this. It was her husband's next words that sealed the deal.

"I was thinking that one of the extra chairs could be thought of in this way: Most of the time, it will probably be unoccupied. What if we considered the chairs in any of these ways?" Jack paused and began to count on his fingers, as if to keep track of his thoughts. "One, as an empty chair for the Lord; two, as an empty chair for baby Jessica; or three, to keep on hand for unexpected guests in keeping with the charism of the Cenacle that 'all are welcome at the table.'"

Like most people, there were moments in Sarah's life that left her at a loss for words. This was one of those moments because she was deeply moved by her husband's thoughtfulness. She communicated her "Yes" by nodding her head, and as she did this, she smiled as her eyes swelled with tears. Thus, the Peterson tradition of "The Extra Chair" was birthed—not on a wing, but definitely on a prayer.

Sunday Dinner at the Peterson's

It is difficult for Jack and Sarah to be away from their family for so many months each winter, but since Sarah doesn't do well in the cold weather, the sacrifice is made.

Although March 17th had passed, Jack and Sarah's "guests" began to arrive for the St. Patrick's Day feast. Since Sarah's ancestors were from Ireland (as were Amy's husband Don's), the family looked forward to this celebration each year with the utmost enthusiasm. "The Extra (empty) Chair" sat silently, reverently even, on the side of the hutch as usual, while the Peterson clan occupied the rest of the chairs—one after the other. "When Irish Eyes are Smiling" was happily playing on the stereo.

Their reasons for celebrating were compounded by the fact that they would also celebrate Sarah and Lillian's birthdays. Each year, when everyone sings, "Happy Birthday, dear Mom and Lily," Jack and Sarah also sneak in Michael, Don, and Rosalie's names because their birthdays had come and gone while they were down south. Simultaneously, all would shout out "Dad/Grandpa" because Jack's birthday had also gone by while they were away. All the extra names threw off the song, but no one cared. So much to celebrate; so much for which to be grateful.

The Happy Birthday song had just concluded when, out of the blue, Rose blurted out, "Nannie, I am sorry you lost your BFF!" Understanding only by context, Sarah thanked little Rose who has such a beautiful heart. Turning to her daughter, Sarah discreetly asked for clarification. After Monica provided her mother with the interpretation of the acronym, she smiled in total agreement because yes, it's true: Gloria Morelli was her "best friend forever" indeed.

Despite the momentary sadness that accompanied Rose's condolences, the home was filled with much joy and laughter. Adding to the excitement were the various shades of green, which were splashed throughout the room amongst the family's clothing, balloons, and jewelry. The table was adorned with Keith's festive bouquet consisting of green carnations, white roses, and a rather large, pale-green bow with flecks of silver adorning the top of the wicker basket. Numerous dark green metallic shamrocks, which had been inserted throughout the bouquet, completed the arrangement. These shamrocks complemented the white and green fine bone china, which adorned the table, and Sarah's mother's stemware featuring the Claddagh symbol also added to the richness of their tradition. All were beautifully and strategically placed on the lovely lace table cloth.

Jack Peterson raised his glass and wished everyone a Happy St. Patrick's Day, and all responded in kind. As per their family tradition, everyone settled down in silence as their family patriarch prayerfully proceeded to read *An Irish Blessing* over his family. Everyone listened reverently, receiving the gift of Jack's prayer.

After a few minutes, Amy posed the following question to everyone: "Who would like some Irish Soda bread?"

It was Jack who answered first, "Amy, I cannot refuse the fruit of your culinary expertise, which thus far has proven exemplary!" Everyone laughed at Jack's elaborate choice of words. Jack is such an amiable, amusing man, and the Petersons are very fortunate to have him as their patriarch.

It was Amy's son, Patrick, who added another layer of laughter to the conversation. Raising his arms to emphasize the upcoming, dramatic, affect, he said as though he were royalty, "Thank you, Grandpa, Nannie, Mom and Dad, for throwing me, *Patrick*, this wonderful party and naming it 'St. Patrick's Day Dinner!' It was so very good of you all to attend."

The responses to his silly, almost-fake expression of gratitude ranged from "Oh, brother," to "*Oy vey!*" to "What in the world am I going to do with you, Patrick?" Vast as the responses were, they were all given in love.

The reunion took off from there.

Deacon Josh, a True Beacon

Deacon Josh had been called to the diaconate around twelve years ago. When the stirrings of the call became too loud to ignore, he and his wife, Christine, spent a great deal of time praying to discern the next steps. They received several confirmations, as well as extraordinary graces, all of which confirmed the stirrings. Grateful for Christine's support, he was ordained several years after the initial call. In addition to the ordinary services of a deacon, his ministry developed into offering retreat work at his home parish, Holy Family, as well as throughout the diocese. He also assists the Eucharistic Ministers if they are unable to keep their appointments to bring communion to the homebound; this is how he had initially met Gloria Morelli.

Everyone in the congregation loves that Deacon Josh embodies the true meaning of the word, deacon, *diakonos* in the Greek: one who serves. He lives out his life in this way, not only on Sundays, but Monday through Saturday, too. To that end, when Deacon Josh found out that the Petersons would be returning home from down south, he requested a day off from work because he surmised Sarah would want to meet with him. He planned to address some much-needed errands and meet with her on the same day. When, as expected, he received Sarah's call, he asked if she could meet on Tuesday morning, and she said, "Yes."

When Sarah arrived at his office, Deacon Josh was unsure if the tiredness he observed was due to the travel or her loss, but he made the assumption that it was probably a combination of both. Sarah expressed her gratitude to Deacon Josh, then proceeded to share with him her sadness, disappointment, and concerns surrounding the loss of her best friend.

The good deacon gave her the space to talk, remaining very emotionally present to his guest. He knew all too well that there was not much he could do or say to alleviate her pain, but nonetheless, he did his best to listen. His presence was the gift he offered her, all the while knowing he was standing on holy ground.

After she seemed to have finished processing her emotions, he thought it appropriate to share the last encounter he had had with Gloria, knowing this might offer Sarah comfort. Deacon Josh explained that he had held an evening retreat at the parish last December and that Gloria had attended. "I'm sorry I was not able to be there," was all Sarah could think to share as she pictured her elderly friend making her way to the church on a cold December evening to participate. She knew the cold weather worsened Gloria's arthritis.

"I would be more than happy to lend you my notes from the talk if you feel that they would in some way help you feel included with the retreat and connect you with Gloria. I know that you and Gloria almost always attended such events together. Would you like that, Mrs. Peterson?"

"Yes, Deacon Josh, I most certainly would," Sarah replied as a tear gently caressed her cheek. Sarah reached for a tissue from the box, which had been appropriately and strategically positioned on his desk. Deacon Josh had learned a long time ago that it is better to leave a tissue box within the reach of his guests as opposed to handing one to them. It was his hope that this would prevent individuals from in any way feeling as if they are a burden to him. Neither did he want to imply that tears make him feel uncomfortable.

Josh went to his file cabinet and pulled out the notes he had prepared for the Advent Retreat, extending them to Sarah. As he offered them to her, he said a quick, silent prayer that she be blessed by them.

Sarah had spent about one hour with this thoughtful man and noticed that some of her grief had diminished and her sense of peace had been restored a bit. Her awareness then turned to her overall condition, and she realized that she was leaving the same way she had come to the meeting—in sheer gratitude.

In the Image of the Divine Gardener

When Sarah returned home after her meeting with Deacon Josh, she planned to look for the essay Keith had written about God and gardening, which he had recently asked her to find. She asked Jack to help her find it, and he said he knew exactly where it was. This surprised her because usually, it was she who knew where everything was, and it was *her husband* who needed *her* assistance in finding them. She is always so grateful for her husband.

Jack went to the den, located the essay, and brought it back to the living room. "Would you like to read it together?" he posed.

"That would be wonderful, Dear," was Sarah's sweet response. "It would be very nice if you would read it out loud. Then we can both benefit."

"Sure, Sarah. No problem."

"Thank you, Jacob."

Every now and again, Sarah refers to her husband by his legal name, Jacob Kent Peterson; Jack is actually his nickname. Few know this little-known fact, yet, of course, his children are aware of it. Keith, knowing his Bible history, is glad his father's real name is Jacob because it worked well within the context of his essay. By referring to "Jacob," he was able to creatively reference his dad and simultaneously make an implication to the Biblical patriarchs, Abraham, Isaac, and Jacob.

Jacob, aka Jack, put on his reading glasses and proceeded to read the poignant essay very carefully and rather slowly. Keith had written the essay when he was in his early twenties after returning home from a Bible study. His father had read it so many times since then that he had a perfect rhythm by which he read it. In addition to expressing Keith's gratitude to God, the powerful composition touches on Creation, gardening, and even redemption history. Keith is just as creative as a writer as he is a gardener, and one can clearly see his artistic expression exhibited in the essay. The subject of the Bible study was the Book of Genesis, and thus, we "begin."

In the Image of the Divine Gardener

I am Adam. I did not work my way through the birth canal. I was formed by my Father, who took lumps of clay and fashioned me in His Image. I am made in the Image of the Divine Gardener. The breath of life was bestowed into me, and I responded with an exhalation. Inspired by Love, I came to life. Gasps swirled among the heavens, "Which is which?" they asked. So much so made in the Image of God—the angels could not tell the difference. *"Imago Dei. Imago Dei,"* they sang across time, their song still floating somewhere across the universe.

I am Adam, only one of two who were created; we were not birthed, yet we were born of God. The second is Eve, Crown of all

Creation, "bone of my bones, and flesh of my flesh." We knew no hardships; we only knew one another and God. *Yada. Yada.* God *knew* us, and we *knew* Him.

I am Adam, the one who was told about the forbidden tree yielding pleasant, but forbidden, fruit. I am he who stood beside her and allowed her crown to be stripped of her. She wasn't there when I was given the instructions (Genesis 2:15–18). She relied on me to know. I stood there as she ate. She took from the "good side" of the tree. She deemed it good, but it was not good. She made a mistake, but it was I who committed treason. I heard Him calling, "*Adamah, mi eifo atta?* Adam, where are you?"

What have I done? What have I done? In His mercy, we must leave the Garden. I carelessly blamed her as we went, and she screamed. Her voice was so loud it seemed to pierce my virgin eardrums. I'm sure her words still ricochet somewhere out in the black hole. *Oy vey!* Birthed from the trauma was her need for control because I wasn't there when she needed me the most. But I *was* there. *I* was there. It was our Garden, and I was there.

The next generation was birthed. I watched as she bore my sons in anguish—two boys each made in *my* image. Though they, too, were made in the Image of God, they did not resemble God in the way that I had.

I heard no angels' voices. I watched the birth of another son, Seth, but I still don't quite understand what happened to his older brother. Now it is *I* asking the same question to *my* son, "Abel, *mi eifo atta?* Abel, where are you?" I heard cries emanating from the earth (Genesis 4:10), through which I had come into being. *Abel, is that you?*

What have I done? What have I done? This question haunted me all the days that followed. I want to go back to the Garden, but there's no "back" to go to. I am stopped by cherubim and a flaming sword turning in every direction (Genesis 3:24). "By the sweat of your brow," He said. *What is sweat?* "Thorns," He said. *What are thorns? What have I done? What have I done? Dear God, what have I done?*

I spent a lifetime trying to make my way back to the Garden in the hopes of reclaiming my true Image of God. To all of mankind, "Please forgive me."

* * *

I am the second Adam. I am the Son of Man. My Father knew me while I was being formed in my mother's womb. *Yada. Yada.* I am made in the Image of the Divine Gardener. I breathe the breath of life. I am Life. I am made in the Divine Image of God. I am the visible image of the invisible God.

I am the last Adam. I am the Son of God.

My Father and I are one. Before Abraham was, I am. I hear the screams of Eve echoing across time; I witnessed her husband's silence. I saw her son betray his brother; I warned Cain that sin was crouching at his door, but he ignored my plea. I hear Abel's blood crying out from the earth, which I created...from the very dirt through which his father came. For this and more, I have come. I am Divine through my Father and human through my mom.

I am the last Adam, born of the Father before all ages. I am He. I am the One for whom you have waited. I am the Christ. Of me, it is written, "The first man, Adam, became a living being; *the last Adam*, a life-giving spirit." I am Spirit; I am Truth. Of you, it is written, "And just as we have borne the image of the earthly man, so shall we bear the image of the heavenly man." It is I, the heavenly man. I am He, the last Adam. It is my heavenly image that you bear deep within your earthly shell.

Father, what am I to do? What am I to do? I must make it right. What must I do? This question is always on my mind. *Your will Father, not mine. What am I to do?*

Of me, it is written, "He is a man of sorrows." For you, I shed all three—blood, sweat, and tears. They crowned me with the very thorns. "'What thorns?' *Those* thorns."

Of me, it is written, "For He *became* sin who knew no sin to *be* sin," Of you, it is written, "for us that we might *become* the righteousness of God in Him." The Great Exchange. It is not your righteousness, it is mine. It is a gift, which I give unto you, and is yours for the taking.

* * *

I am Keith, son of Jacob, birthed by Sarah. Tarnished by the sins of the first Adam, redeemed by the second, and there shall be no third. I have committed my own sins. "And whosoever shall keep the whole law, but offend in one point, is become guilty of all" (James 2:10). Yet, I am redeemed by Grace. "The whole creation has been groaning as in the pains of childbirth right up to the present time" (Romans 8:22). As part of Creation, I, too, groan for when all is restored to right order.

I am Keith, a gardener. I am told my name means "wood." This makes me think of trees. In the very first Garden, there was a forbidden tree. It didn't go well. Then a savior hung on a tree, the last Adam, and this has made all the difference. Both trees displayed both good and evil. The first tree met with Adam's disobedience. The second one, the cross, was met with the obedience of Christ.

I am Keith; I harvest flowers. Create me in the Image of the Divine Gardener, and help me harvest souls for Your kingdom.

Of me, it is written, "for us that we might

become the righteousness of God in Him."
I am the righteousness of God in Christ;
praise God. A sinner saved by Grace; praise
God. A sinner turned saint; praise God.

I, Keith, together with all who have come
before me, and even those who will come
after me, await the second coming of the
second Adam. He will bring us back home.
He will bring us back to the Garden. He will
bring us back to the Tree of Life because
he draws us back unto Himself. Amen.

Essential: [adjective] of, or relating to

Although the commonality that drew Keith and Barbara together was their interest in flowers, Barbara's appreciation of them is less well known. Much like her husband, she is fascinated by the Book of Genesis, which contains her favorite Scripture, Genesis 1:29: "Then God said, 'I give you every seed-bearing plant on the face of the whole earth and every tree that has fruit with seed in it. They will be yours for food.'" As a teenager, Barbara was able to see that flowers and trees offer unique gifts, and she turned her interest into both a career and a hobby. She is a botanist who works at the local arboretum.

Barbara's interest in botany began in her tenth-grade biology class when she learned a seemingly elementary concept. This commonly known scientific fact turned out to be the impetus for her desire to learn more. Her biology teacher introduced the class to the process known as photosynthesis, and she was, and continues to be, fascinated that plants utilize sunlight, water, and carbon dioxide to manufacture food. She distinctly remembers learning that water goes up the xylem and, after converting to chlorophyl, goes down the phloem as food to nourish the plant. Nourishment is a key word in her vocabulary.

In her spare time, and as a hobby, Barbara has also amassed a great deal of knowledge concerning essential oils and their therapeutic benefits. Essential oils have been harvested for millennia for flavoring and for the extraction of their healing properties, amongst many other uses. As anointing oils, they have been used to anoint kings as well as to anoint the sick. Any way Barbara looks at essential oils, she is intellectually intrigued and enjoys discovering their unique qualities, as well as the various methods used to collect the oils. She also enjoys learning about the places from which they originate and the farmers who harvest them.

Most of all, Barbara absolutely loves their use as aromatherapy with some of her favorite scents being bergamot, spearmint, and frankincense. Keith appreciates the smell of lemon oil and Rose and Lily particularly enjoy spearmint and lavender, respectively. The family knows that they need to use the potent oils with care.

When they adopted Charity, Barbara explained that some essential oils are unsafe to use around cats, so they are even more careful with their use. They have even had to stop using many of the oils altogether.

For as long as Barbara can remember, she shared her hobby with Gloria Morelli whom she had met when she was in her early twenties. Since Gloria's passing, Barbara has missed spending time with her. She can still remember when her then-boyfriend, Keith, introduced her to Miss Gloria. Gloria immediately loved her godson's girlfriend, and, in typical Gloria Morelli fashion, she took her in with open arms. After having introduced Miss Gloria to her love of essential oils, she and Barbara spent many hours talking about them, and neither ever grew tired of it. Oftentimes, when Barbara went to visit Miss Gloria, she would bring her case full of the oils; Miss Gloria would have her Bible.

Combining their two loves, the women would search the Bible for passages, which referenced ancient oils. Barbara welcomed the opportunity to share her collection of aromatic oils with her friend, and inhaling the scents mentioned throughout Scripture brought the Bible to life in new and incredible ways.

Some of the Scriptures they studied, which made reference to the exotic oils, fragrances, and perfumes included: Exodus 30:22–33; 1 Samuel 16:12–13; Esther 2:12; Song of Songs 1:3, 4:10; Ezekiel 47:12; Matthew 2:11; John 12:3; and Revelation 22:1–2, just to name a few. But of all the Scripture passages they discussed, Psalm 45:8 always remained Gloria's favorite because combining the scents of myrrh and cassia combined with aloe created one of the most beautiful aromas she had ever experienced. Barbara knew how much Gloria loved the scent, so she created a heartwarming candle and gave it to her. Because of the candle, it was easy for Gloria to detect the scent of Jesus' robes, both on earth and now in Heaven.

Recognizing Barbara's love of these treasures, Gloria purchased a wall plaque for her with the following quote taken from a book Gloria had been given as a little girl, *Le Petit Prince* by Antoine de Saint Exupéry:

"L'essentiel est invisible pour les yeux."

Since Barbara did not speak French, Miss Gloria happily offered the translation: "What is essential is invisible to the eyes." It was easy to see how Gloria, the wordsmith, used this quote as a play on words. Gloria knew it would resonate with Barbara because of the word "essential," and she was hoping it would evoke a desire in her to contemplate the true meaning of life and its treasures.

Each of the women adored their gifts, but each adored one another even more.

A Grave, but Good Day

Sarah planned to bring the two bouquets she had been given to the cemetery. She didn't mind sharing them; besides, this would still leave her and Jack with the beautiful St. Patrick's Day arrangement on the dining room table. The bouquet, with its many shamrocks and fresh carnations and roses, is a tangible, fragrant reminder of all the fun they had had during their wonderful reunion.

She would leave the "Welcome Home" bouquet from Monica on baby Jessica's grave. She attached a note to the bouquet from Keith and would leave it on Gloria's fresh grave. Her handwritten note captured the sentiments she now feels regarding their friendship. The quote was taken from her favorite saint, St. Françis de Sales: "Friendships begun in this world will be taken up again, never to be broken off."

It took Sarah a few days to prepare emotionally to go to the cemetery. On Friday, she and Jack finally headed out with the bouquets. The cemetery was next to a beautiful park, so Sarah packed a picnic lunch for them to eat after their visit. It was a beautiful day, and the weather was almost Edenic. Sarah also brought along a portable CD player and a specific CD, which she wanted to play when she visited her daughter's grave. The CD contained a particular track, which had helped Sarah process the death of their baby girl. The song, entitled "One Small Star," seemed to capture the vast range of emotions that dwell within her soul.

They visited Jessica's grave first and then made their way to Gloria's. This was an extremely difficult experience, but both knew they needed to visit the place where Gloria's body quietly awaits the Resurrection. It was so peaceful as they stood there taking it all in. Jack placed the bouquet nearby the headstone that read, "Gentle Gloria, friend of God." As Sarah looked with sadness at the words, she found herself staring at the same date she had just seen on Jessica's tombstone, "December 11." It occurred to her that Gloria died on the very date Jessica had been born. She surmised that part of the reason Jack probably did not want to tell her about Gloria's death while they were down south was because he knows that Jessica's birthday is always an already pensive day for her.

After a short while, Sarah whispered a faint, "Goodbye, Gloria. We'll see you again."

"Indeed, we will, Love," Jack responded in agreement. He, too, whispered, "Goodbye," to Gloria as he gently took his wife's hand. They turned away and headed towards the car as their focus began to be drawn to their picnic lunch. It was Jack who first noticed the beautiful display off yonder in the distance. Out of nowhere, a beautiful rainbow appeared in the sky, reminding them of God's promises. The subtle rainbow seemed to ease the desolation they were feeling.

With the rainbow as their canopy, Jack hugged his wife as if to reiterate the words he had said when he first told her of Gloria's passing. They seemed to be the same words the simple, silent rainbow was conveying, "It'll be okay, Sarah. It'll be okay."

Meanwhile, right this very minute, on the other side of town, their son, Keith, was kneeling in his garden planting the spring bulbs, which would bloom in early summer. As he was working, he paused momentarily to inhale the fresh, robust smell of the dirt. Taking a deep breath, he looked up, and as he did, he, too, caught sight of the beautiful, elusive rainbow! Awestruck and humbled by its translucent beauty, he spontaneously blurted out the first words that popped into his head, "Genesis 9:13!"

Though he did not know it, he was not alone in the garden as he worked, and, to the angels that stood by him, it appeared that his words had been addressed to God, given he was kneeling, as if in prayer.

Consolations and Desolations

Earlier in the year, Monica began facilitating a group for women who were in need of emotional support. Over the eight-week period, some of her clients expressed their belief that life had "passed them by," while others felt invisible or alone. One participant, Jane, even went so far as to say that she believed God had forgotten about her. Monica recognized the spiritual desolation Jane was experiencing and did her best to honor where Jane was while simultaneously highlighting the many graces, which proved otherwise. As the sessions advanced, the group was very pleased to hear that Jane could see that her belief was untrue and that God had been present with her at all times.

During the opening session, Monica had encouraged the women to express their emotions in their own unique, personal ways by inviting them to draw or paint pictures. While some chose to express their feelings through artwork, others chose to write down their thoughts. One woman decided to make a list of all the people who had hurt her in an effort to forgive them one by one, while another chose to process her pain through poetry. Monica also invited them to share their work with the group if they felt comfortable doing so.

Some of the drawings and paintings that were brought to

the sessions seemed to confirm the old adage, "A picture speaks a thousand words." One of the women, Alison, decided to draw pictures of angels. The drawing that touched Monica most deeply was the initial one Alison had drawn, which she brought to the second session; it was an angel bent over in exhaustion, and Alison explained through her tears that she thought that perhaps even her guardian angel was tired from the journey. The angst which the drawing portrayed resonated with most of the women, and a deep trust was established among the circle as each shared their response to this image and what it evoked deep within their hearts.

Monica and the other women were amazed to see how the angel pictures that Alison brought to subsequent sessions seemed to be cheerful, reflecting her commitment towards her own inner healing. All the women agreed that it might help Alison to sit and pray with all four of the angel drawings, and so she did.

Alison was both surprised and pleased that her new-found friends liked the drawings so much that she went to the library to make enough copies for each of the women in the circle, including Monica. As the facilitator, it occurred to Monica that it might be a good idea for Alison to name each of her drawings. Alison said that she could not think of an appropriate enough name for the first one, but was able to name the remaining three. Her titles were as follows:

I will watch over you

Flowers from Heaven

Kneel alongside me, the best is yet to be

It was very heartwarming for Monica to witness how the women encouraged and affirmed one another. Through this sense of community and belonging, the women became more confident and hopeful. Despite the emerging hopefulness Monica witnessed growing among the women, she found herself experiencing some type of spiritual desolation after having heard many heartbreaking stories over the course of the eight weeks, which she attributed to second-hand grief.

Monica planned to go to the nearby arboretum on Saturday morning to sit among the spring flowers to see if this would help ease the desolation she was feeling. At the last minute, she decided to bring Alison's angel pictures and pray with them as well.

Monica found a peaceful place under an old oak tree. After settling down on the bench, which was shaded by the ancient tree's vast limbs, she took out her journal. Admiring the beauty of the grounds seemed to quiet her mind. Her emotions and longings began to reveal themselves as she began to pray, using Alison's pictures as a way to enter the prayer. The fourth picture, the kneeling angel, prompted a stirring in her heart. The stirrings turned to thoughts, which ultimately landed on the pages of the journal, as "Little Saint Monica" penned the following words from her time of contemplation:

> Dearest God, Creator of all living things, restore life to Your Creation. As I witness others cautiously and courageously emerge from the imagined safety of the protective walls they have known, some crawling out of darkened caves towards Your light, I am no longer able to ignore the existence of suffering. I am beginning to see how desperately we need You down here.

I sense the pleading from a lost soul who seeks to injure the body that houses it, the very body that You provided for that soul. The very body that You knit together before time began. The wound is bleeding and is crying out, "Help me, I am frightened, I feel alone with the rage that courses through my very core"— vandalism at its worst because the anger has imploded. No one seems to notice the cut because most are caught up in the drudgery of life. All is not well in the world.

I hear fear in the voice of another who received a report from the doctor that could go either way. She was told they found something. Let her find faith, which is greater than the physically-manifested soul sickness, which the doctors found. Restore her to wholeness, Oh God; she so needs You down here.

I cry as I realize the overwhelming sense of loneliness that befriends another. Addictions keep it at bay, but the loneliness leaches onto the soul like a dreaded limb, too heavy to carry, yet too elusive to identify. I pray that You fill this aching soul with love, truth, and joy in abundance. You are so desperately needed down here!

I think of my older women friends who are widows, whose husbands have returned to Your kingdom. They share the wisdom of the crone years with me, and we share moments of fleeting laughter. They, too, are lonely and seek consolation and protection from You because they miss their husbands and all is not the way they had planned in their worlds.

Jesus was present to provide His healing balm of love and truth to wounds so deep only He—the Man of Sorrows—could redefine and heal them. Amidst the tears and hugs, we shared smiles. Thank you for your abundant love. Thank you for giving them beauty for ashes. Thank you for planting flowers to enliven and beautify the barren desert fields that had eroded each of their souls for far too long.

I know the grief and anguish of the clients in my circle, a sacred bond of sisterhood. Hearing the cries of their hearts and knowing the depths of the buried suffering has not been easy for me.

I experience the longing in my own spirit that needs to hold Your hand forever and to be enveloped in the comfort of Your embrace. Amidst the cacophony of noise, tireless haste, and overwhelming difficulties, I anchor my soul to Your love and beg You to keep me safe among the raging seas. Your steadfast

love is the mooring to which I tie my life.
Father God, I need You so desperately
down here.

I begin to contemplate how far You went
to be with Your Creation. Jesus died a
painful death, feeling abandoned and
forsaken. His body was broken for all
of this and more. Your heart was broken for every abuse You witnessed, for
every tear that we have shed, for every
offense, and for every injustice. You
loved us even when we were "dead in
our transgressions." Jesus asked You
to forgive us because we were too blind
to see the truth.

And as much as we so desperately need
You down here, You have with greater
desire always so desperately wanted us
to be with You up there, safe above
the storms, high above the heartache,
in the eternal Heavenly realm where every tear is wiped away and where, in the
fullness of time, we shall see the face
of God.

Monica read her own reflection and could sense a spirit of consolation emerging as she began to see that her work
was truly making a difference in the lives of others. It almost
seemed as if the Lord Himself were thanking her, and she, in
turn, was grateful for His gratitude. She sat for a long time after having been given this consolation and was deep in thought
when she noticed a woman approaching from the distance.

As the woman got closer, she realized it was Theresa, another woman who had attended the group.

"Oh, hi Monica," she said as she hesitantly approached.

"Good morning, Theresa. How are you? Isn't this weather perfect?"

"I find it a bit chilly for this time of year. Weather like this refreshes my soul!" Theresa replied.

Whenever Monica runs into a client outside of the office, she never brings up anything that was discussed in the privacy of their sacred space; however, if the client brings something up, she is willing to entertain the conversation a bit. Theresa shared how helpful the eight weeks had been for her, and she also told Monica that she had recently been given a prayer book, which was written by a Christian author. She asked Monica if she would like to see the book, and, assuming she would, she extended her arm to hand it to her.

Monica was astonished when she opened the pages upon seeing an adorable little sticker placed on the inside cover:

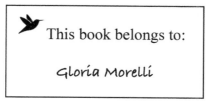

This book belongs to:

Gloria Morelli

Monica was touched by Gloria's beautiful handwriting, which she knew so well. Seeing her signature brought her a combination of joy and nostalgia as she remembered that Gloria's script was like none other. She pointed to the sticker, asking Theresa if she knew Gloria.

"Yes. She was my elderly friend who recently passed away. Her family thought I might like to have the book as a remembrance of her. I'm glad that they gave it to me. It means the world to me. It's one of my treasures. Miss Gloria always pointed out what she treasured."

Recognizing the influence Gloria had apparently had on Theresa and having been reminded that "treasures" were of the utmost importance to Gloria, chills ran down Monica's spine. She could hardly believe she was holding the very same book of poems from which her mom's best friend, Gloria Morelli, must have found comfort! As she handed the book back to her client, a paper fell to the ground. When Monica picked it up, she saw that it was an invitation to the Heavenly Banquet. On the back of the beautiful invitation was Theresa's signature.

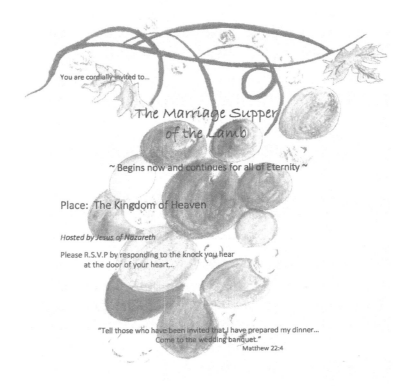

You are cordially invited to...

The Marriage Supper of the Lamb

~ Begins now and continues for all of Eternity ~

Place: The Kingdom of Heaven

Hosted by Jesus of Nazareth

Please R.S.V.P by responding to the knock you hear at the door of your heart...

"Tell those who have been invited that I have prepared my dinner... Come to the wedding banquet."
Matthew 22:4

Unaware of the sea of emotions stirring inside of Monica, Theresa continued, "I was just reading some of the poems while sitting on the other side of the arboretum, and one of them confirmed what I have been learning these past few months." After explaining that she didn't want to intrude, Theresa politely asked, "Would it be okay to share the poem? I'd like to read it to you."

"Of course, Theresa. I would like that very much." After a slight pause, Monica continued, "Theresa, I know you were very quiet during our eight weeks together, and I remember you had mentioned that you were grieving because you had recently lost a good friend. I didn't know it was Gloria. I knew her and loved her, too. I would like to extend my condolences to you again at the loss of your friend."

After Theresa thanked her, Monica followed up with yet another question. Still holding the paper, which had fallen out of the book, she asked, "Theresa, did you create this invitation?"

Gloria's young friend replied humbly, "Yes. I had shared it with her before she passed away. It made her so happy. Now, I often find myself picturing her there at the table in Heaven. That helps ease the pain."

"It's beautiful!"

After thanking Monica again, Theresa proceeded to read the poem aloud to her mentor, which highlighted one's journey into the very heart of God.

Welcome Home
By: Arlene DeMar

Colors ablaze across the landscape of my soul
While laughter dances her way into a place, she longed to
    discover ~
Fluffy clouds of white gently sail on winds of Peace...

And the grass grows softly in the Silence that surrounds her.

No storm clouds ~ neither hint of yesterday's pain ~ just
    promises of bright tomorrows
preceded only by the Stillness of today's warmth.

The bird sings a joyful song as she nestles in the trees that
    keep her safe.
A flower softly sways as the breezes of love carry her
    sweet fragrance,
and she knows at once that she is Deeply Loved.

And suddenly, it occurs to me this place existed all the while
    within me.
I just needed to close my eyes, to open them there, in order
    to see.
And all the colors, and all the joy, and all the peace,
and all the rest of it are all God indwelling the very places
    He created ~
and there He is in the midst of me.

And without hesitation, without question, without reserve,
Yet with Great Love and a feeling of finally being home,
I clearly see that there I am, too, in the midst of Him.

It is there I hear Him declaring,
"Welcome home, my love, welcome home."

Monica thanked Theresa for sharing the poem; Theresa
thanked Monica for taking the time to listen. Theresa turned
to go and as she did, Monica's eyes began to tear up because
once again, she realized the positive effect she was having on

others. She could also see that her mother's friend, Miss Gloria, continues to help others even though she herself is in Heaven.

Monica wondered if it was God who had led Theresa to her now to confirm the stirrings she was sensing of His gratitude. She could also sense the spiritual desolation abating and spiritual consolation taking its place. She sat still under the shade of the oak tree until she felt ready to leave the sacred time and space.

Deacon Josh's Advent Reflection

On Saturday morning, while Monica was visiting the arboretum across town, her mother decided to sit down with the notes Deacon Josh had given her for the Advent Retreat he had hosted last December. Sarah was looking forward to doing so ever since he had graciously shared them with her. *Deacon Josh is truly a quality man*, Sarah thought as she sat on the sofa in the room, which the family referred to as the "Florida Room." It is her favorite room in the house. The room was actually an enclosed patio on the south side of the Peterson's house, and Sarah thought it would be a peaceful place to read it.

The sun warms the cozy room, which has an electric fireplace in it for chillier days. The fireplace allows them to enjoy the room year-round. Sarah wanted to put the fireplace on to help set the mood, as if she were actually attending an Advent Retreat on a cold December day. Besides, even though it was late March, there was a bit of a chill in the air today.

Sarah had told Jack all about the "retreat" she would be making this morning, and, hearing the unusual circumstances, he wanted to help her prepare for the mini retreat. Jack put the fireplace on, turning the heat selection to a low setting. The blazing "fire" is always a warm and welcoming sight. He then went to the kitchen to prepare a cup of hot chocolate for her to help simulate a frosty, winter day. He was so happy when he found a few marshmallows in the cabinet; Sarah always enjoys them in a cup of hot chocolate along with a single drop of peppermint oil. Jack looked forward to surprising his bride with the drink.

Quieting her mind, Sarah began to read Deacon Josh's notes, imagining his reading them last December to the retreatants, one of whom was her "BFF," Gloria Morelli.

<u>Advent...a Time of Waiting</u>

As winter slowly makes her way into our lives again, the days are getting shorter and the darkness settles in earlier each evening. During this Holy Advent Season, we wait. Waiting for Christmas, we again prepare to celebrate the birth of our Savior and this includes reflecting.

Our wondering may lead us to ponder how it might have been for the Angel Gabriel as he waited for Mary's "Yes," or what "waiting" meant for the people in Jesus' life. At that time, all the Jewish people were waiting for their Messiah! Reflecting on Mary and Joseph and how they may have waited, I envision Joseph waiting courageously and confidently for the fulfillment of a promise made known to him in a dream. I imagine Mary prayerfully waiting—day by day— while Life was growing inside her womb. The "old man" Simeon waited a lifetime to see his Savior's face–what a day that must have been to at last behold the face of God! And God Himself waited until the fullness of time to bring forth the Divine birth that changed all of history.

Even within this Advent Wreath, there is a sense of waiting…

(PURPLE CANDLE) The first candle on the wreath, which was lit this past Sunday, is a symbol of **hope**. Proverbs 13 tells us that, "Hope deferred makes the heart sick, but when the desire comes, it is a tree of life;" and the psalmist in Psalm 130 sings, "I wait for the Lord, my whole being waits, and in his word I put my hope." We always have this confidence: we wait not as those who are hopeless, but as those who have a Great Hope.

(PURPLE CANDLE) We will light the second candle on the wreath in just a few days. It represents **preparation**. Preparation encompasses "waiting" because the fruit of a harvest is not yet realized during the time of preparation. Preparation time is seed-planting time so it is good to pray for the graces that we will need as the seeds are germinating.

(ROSE CANDLE) The third candle on the wreath is a symbol of joy. The angels spoke of this glorious **joy** when they declared, "I bring you good tidings of great joy that will be for all the people." And that is what we are invited to ponder and experience during the third week of Advent: JOY, unspeakable joy.

(PURPLE CANDLE) The fourth candle, which represents **love**, will be lit on the Sunday before Christmas, and of course, what does the Bible say about love? "It is patient and kind." And doesn't patience also imply waiting?

All of these themes, of course, are collectively embodied in the liturgy throughout the year when the priest proclaims each week, "Deliver us, Lord, from every evil, and grant us peace in our day. In Your mercy keep us free from sin and safe from all distress as we wait in joyful hope for the coming of our Savior, Jesus Christ."

We can contemplate waiting in many different ways. For instance…

Do you find yourself waiting *on* God, *for* God, or are you waiting *with* God?

Are you waiting *on* God for an answer? Are you waiting *on* God for relief? Are you waiting *on* God to receive healing for you or a loved one? "Waiting *on* God" is fruitful as the Bible tells us in Isaiah 40:31:

But those who *wait on the Lord*

Shall renew their strength;
They shall mount up with wings like eagles,
They shall run and not be weary,
They shall walk and not faint.

Are you waiting *for* God to answer a prayer or to provide guidance, or are you waiting *for* God to speak? Then again, maybe you're like me and waiting eagerly *for* the second coming of Christ in these last days.

Referring again to Psalm 130, verse 6 says, "I wait *for* the LORD more than watchmen for the morning—more than watchmen wait for the morning." This conjures up images of darkness and light, which are also major themes of Advent. It also speaks to the sense of eagerness with which the psalmist waits for God. The Hebrew words for "wait" and "hope" encompass an element of expectation that the English translation does not convey.

Perhaps you are waiting *with* God in chaos or even better—in the Silence. Perhaps you are waiting *with* God during a season of grieving or loss. More often than not, God's timing is very different from ours, so learning to wait *with* God is a necessary part of the journey.

~ Regardless of the manner in which you wait, are you feeling God's love in that place? ~

Note: At this point, invite retreatants to find a solitary place to journal and reflect. We will reconvene in 45 minutes in the sanctuary for a time of sharing.

After time of sharing, play "O Holy Night" and dismiss.

* * *

Sarah sat for a long while processing Deacon Josh's thoughts, which had touched her deeply. Much was stirring, and she would remain in the Florida Room for a while to sort out her own thoughts. It was nice to be able to experience her own version of the retreat that Gloria had attended on the Wednesday night before she passed away. Sarah felt very connected to her friend in this regard. She contemplated that if she had been home last December, she would have attended the evening retreat with her friend; this was a nice alternative, at least, given the circumstances.

Sarah's thoughts paused as she glanced out the window. She was concentrating so much on last winter that she thought she was imagining snow gently falling. She sat there awhile "imagining" the snow but then came to realize that it wasn't her imagination after all! Even though it was late March, snow, albeit not much, was gently falling outside. How peaceful it appeared as it gently landed on the beautiful spring daffodils that were in her view. Falling snow always reminds Sarah of the poem by Robert Frost, "Stopping by Woods on a Snowy Evening," and she was comforted as the poem, which she had memorized long ago, drifted like the snow itself through her memories:

Whose woods these are, I think I know,
His house is in the village though,
he will not see me standing here
To watch his woods fill up with snow...

So much has happened in one week, Sarah thought as she realized it was only last Saturday that Amy had picked them up at the train station. This revelation turned her attention again to "returning home," and, recalling her dream about Gloria, she envisioned Gloria's homecoming. This thought brought Sarah joy because, although she had no idea what that looked like in actuality, she knew it would have been beautiful.

Another thing Sarah knew for sure is that her answer to the last question, which Deacon Josh had posed to the retreatants, "Regardless of the manner in which you wait, are you feeling God's love in that place?" is an unwavering, "Yes."

Contemplating the Lord's love and care turned her attention to Amy and her deep assimilation of God's love, which guided her daughter's spiritual journey.

Three Carmelite Women

Introduced to hagiography by her older sister, Amy is fascinated to see how individuals from one tradition learned from those in other traditions and how the men and women influenced one another across the 'religious orders.' It was Monica who taught Amy that St. Françis de Sales was highly influenced by his Jesuit education. She also taught her that both St. Thérèse of Lisieux, a Carmelite, and St. Vincent de Paul of the Vincentians were very much influenced by Salesian Spirituality. Monica believes that these influences point directly to the very heart of Jesus and His desire for unity as expressed in His Sacerdotal Prayer in John 17.

Since Amy is a contemplative at heart, she resonates most closely with Carmelite Spirituality. She is intrigued by two particular Carmelite women, both of whom are doctors of the church—St. Teresa of Avila, a Spanish Carmelite who lived during the sixteenth century and St. Thérèse of Lisieux, a nineteenth-century Carmelite. So enamored by these two prayerful women, Amy decided after much prayer and discernment to join the Third Order of Our Lady of Mount Carmel. As a Lay Carmelite, she enjoys being in fellowship with others who admire and learn from these heroes of the faith, as well as others such as St. John of the Cross. Carmelite Spirituality has a special devotion to Mary, the Mother of God, and this allows Amy to deepen her own.

Many years ago, Amy Peterson-McDermott, the Lay

Carmelite, prepared a reflection on St. Teresa. She decided to make copies of it for her fellow lay sisters in the hopes of sharing what she had learned and inspiring their walk with God. Much to her delight, each recipient always expresses gratitude for her willingness to share.

St. Teresa of Avila, for Whom *"God Alone Is Enough"*

Christians are invited to have an authentic, *experiential* knowledge of God whereby we will, "grasp how wide and long and high and deep is the love of Christ, and (come) to know this love that surpasses knowledge" (Ephesians 3:18–19). Paradoxically, we are called to know that which surpasses what we are capable of knowing! Yet, despite this, we see this hunger to know God in the life of Teresa of Avila. Teresa generously gives us a glimpse of her intimate relationship with God. When you read her writings, you will see it is clear she struggled to articulate her experiences. The poor woman even wrote while she had a headache. She shared these very personal encounters hoping to have others come to know what is possible.

The door to Teresa's *Interior Castle* is prayer, and a personal relationship with God is paramount for her. She had enough courage to enter the inward journey to the soul. Teresa knows that the King dwells at this "Divine Center." She encourages her sisters to make the (sometimes arduous) journey inward. From across the centuries, we are invited to enter as well.

Teresa introduced the importance for the soul to gain self-knowledge during its initial journey into the castle. She attributes the process of gaining self-knowledge to God's mercy. Doesn't this echo, "You did not choose me, but I chose you" (John 15:16)? Many saints have indicated that there seems to be a reciprocal correlation between knowing one's self and knowing God. St. Augustine spoke of this as well, for instance.

There are three aspects of "knowing," each of which are true. I kept them in mind as I made my way through *The Interior Castle*. There are *things you know you know*, and of course there are *things you know you don't know*. But there are also *things you don't know you don't know*. As I reflected on this last revelation, I realized it is the one that requires the most humility. It is hard for most people to live in the questions. I am still learning how to do this.

As one's walk with God matures, one may come to a deeper understanding of God both intellectually (knowledge of God) and emotionally/experientially. For me, I have attempted to stay very close to Scripture to help me, "grasp how wide and long and high and deep is the love of Christ." This has led me on an inner journey to discover "who Amy is." This desire was confirmed by my elderly friend, Gloria Morelli, who (unprompted by me) has often told me to, "keep discovering who Amy is." In hindsight, my experience, too, echoes the words of both Sts. Teresa and Augustine.

Many sojourners of the historical Christian tradition indicate that amassing knowledge is *not* the goal of the Spiritual journey. The Hebrew word *yada* is translated "to know" and is used throughout the Bible. In Genesis, Adam *knew* Eve (Genesis 4:1), and of Jeremiah we learn that before God formed him in the womb, God *knew* him (Jeremiah 1:5). This ancient word, *yada,* connotes knowing intimately and includes the ability to perceive, to understand, and to know by reflection and revelation. God *knows* each of us in this way.

God is inviting Teresa (and each of us) to *know* God in this way. She was often confident of what she knew, but she also struggled to articulate what she knew and understood to be true from both her earthly and mystical experiences. This dichotomy often drew my mind to the cataphatic and apophatic ways of knowing. The best way to convey my understanding of these terms is by example:

Using the cataphatic way, I can understand God as Father because I know what it means to be a father from my own experience with my dad, but using the apophatic way informs me that although this is helpful to my understanding, it is incomplete because my understanding is limited since *God as Father* is a much deeper, richer experience.

The apophatic way (which translates *via negativa*) denotes that my understanding of an earthly father is negated because the manner in which an earthly dad is father and the manner in which God is Father are vastly different. I suggest there is a Scripture that refers to this disparity: "If you then, though you are evil, know how to give good gifts to your children, *how much more* will your Father in heaven give good gifts to those who ask him!" (Matthew 7:11, *emphasis mine*).

Teresa's ongoing desire to do God's will is evident as she practices humility and renders service—each of these expressions are the fruit of her prayer. The mysticism of both Sts. Ignatius of Loyola and Teresa of Avila expresses the intimate union of the human and divine, and each of them are moved to service for the Kingdom of God. Each mystic comes to know God in unique and beautiful ways.

Like Ignatius who gives all glory to God, Teresa teaches that favors are granted by God, permitting His glory to be known. In the words of St. Ignatius, *"Ad Majorem Dei Gloriam,"* to God be the glory!

Preparing for Easter–
A Lenten Retreat

It is customary for Christian churches to hold evening retreats during Lent in preparation for Easter. Since retreat work is Deacon Josh's ministry, he prepared a reflection for his parish. As tonight's retreat began, he welcomed all who came.

Included among the retreatants were Sarah, Monica, Barbara, and their husbands. Don and Amy were unable to attend because Don had a prior commitment; Amy thought it would be nice to offer to stay home and watch all the Peterson children while the others participated. Her daughter, Patricia, asked to attend the retreat, so before his meeting, Don brought her to Keith and Barbara who happily took her to the church.

The congregation was unusually quiet as all sat waiting for the evening to begin. The silence helped each enter into a state of prayerfulness and openness to what Deacon Josh would say. Despite the silence, there seemed to be a noticeable anticipation. After a few minutes, the evening was underway.

"Good evening to each of you. Thank you so much for coming tonight. Your presence here means a great deal to me, and I'm sure it does to the Lord as well. I thought that I would open our retreat by first speaking of Lent itself—its history, customs, and its meaning. We will then enter into its richness." He opened up in prayer and then began to share his heartfelt reflections:

> Lent originated in the very early days of the church as a preparatory time for Easter. In most churches the colors used for decorations during this season are purple or blue–royal colors to prepare for the King of kings! Lent is a forty-day period, which begins on Ash Wednesday and ends on the day before Easter, Holy Saturday.
>
> Several weeks ago, we received our ashes. While placing ashes on our foreheads in the sign of the cross, the priest spoke words similar to these: "Remember, man, that you are dust and unto dust you shall return." The ashes that the priest used were last year's undistributed palm branches that were since burned. This gesture takes us back to the moment in the Garden of Eden where we stand with Adam and Eve when God reminds Adam after the Fall that his body is dust, and, now that he has fallen, to dust it shall return. Sadly, the human body was no longer eternal. {Note to self: The Scripture reference here is Genesis 3:19.}
>
> On the liturgical calendar, Ash Wednesday is the seventh Wednesday before Easter. And now that we know how the date for Ash Wednesday is determined, how does the church determine when Easter Sunday will be each year? Easter is considered a "moveable feast," which means that it does not occur on the same date every year. The Council of Nicaea (325 AD) set the date for Easter as the Sunday following the paschal full moon, which is the full moon that

falls on or after the vernal (spring) equinox.

As you recall, Fr. Dominick invited us to take a Lenten Journey. Our retreat tonight is part of that journey as each of you has chosen to withdraw from the world this evening and enter into a place where we encounter God more deeply. The theme of this Holy Season, which is now well underway, is retreating into the wilderness with Jesus, and that is where I would like for us to turn our attention. And who better to learn about retreating than from Jesus Himself, our Savior and Lord who immediately after His baptism was led by the Holy Spirit into the desert for forty long days and forty cold nights?

The synoptic gospels of Matthew, Mark, and Luke let us know that, "At once the Spirit sent him out into the wilderness, and he was in the wilderness forty days, being tempted by Satan. He was with the wild animals, and angels attended him." {Note to self: The Scripture reference here is Mark 1:12–13, see also Matthew 4:1, Luke 4:1.}

What is most intriguing about the temptation is that Jesus had just been declared a "Beloved Son," and it is this very identity that is being questioned, not by Jesus, but by the one who tempts Him.

The first temptation: "If You are the Son of God, command that these stones become bread," and of course, Jesus answers, "It is written: 'Man shall not live by bread alone, but by every word that proceeds from the mouth of God'" (NKJV). Jesus has been fasting, he is hungry, and yet, he is still able to withstand the devil's schemes. Note how Jesus quotes the scriptures just like he does to the two on the road to Emmaus on the days between the Crucifixion and the Resurrection. I often think if Jesus is quoting scripture, then that should certainly be my stance! What does that look like for His disciples: Put on the full armor of God, which includes the Sword of the Spirit—the powerful Word of God.

The second temptation has to do with the three "P's," Power, Position, and Prestige: "All this authority I will give You, and their glory; for this has been delivered to me, and I give it to whomever I wish. Therefore, if You will worship before me, all will be Yours," the devil states (Luke 4:6, NKJV). Jesus answers, "Get behind me Satan! For it is written, 'You shall worship the Lord your God, and Him only you shall serve'" (Luke 48). This response demonstrates that Jesus is choosing to hold on to his belovedness rather than to find his identity in the things of this world. This temptation has to do with kingdoms—the earthly one, which he is being offered—and the Kingdom of Heaven, which is already here (at hand) and simultaneously, not yet fully realized.

In the third exchange, the devil tempts Jesus to throw himself down from the temple. Can you imagine? He begins with another "if" clause and continues, "For it is written: 'He shall give His angels charge over you, To keep you,' and 'In their hands they shall bear you up, Lest you dash your foot against a stone.'" Jesus reminds his tempter that "It has been said, 'You shall not tempt the LORD your God'" (Luke 4:12, NKJV). He's speaking directly to the devil, and He says, "*your* God." God is the God of all, even the one who is doing the tempting! Contemplating these exchanges is no easy task.

And so tonight during this Lenten season, we, too, are invited to enter into our own wilderness. During this time, we will pray. We will fast. We are penitential. During our time in the wilderness, we evaluate our lives, our choices, and what is important to us. We turn inward to consider the condition of our hearts, to strengthen our relationship with God (and others) and to remember, that we, too, are called "Beloved" and to allow this truth to permeate our being.

We are not alone; angels minister to us in the wilderness as they ministered to Jesus. And Jesus offers assistance because he knows full well from his own experiences how temptation operates. And it is precisely right here that we need to know that God's strength, "is made perfect in our weakness." Enter God's mercy.

During this Holy Season, we will cry out, "Hosanna!" on Palm Sunday as our King rides into Jerusalem on a donkey. On Holy Thursday, we will share the Last Supper with Him in the upper room, *Cenaculum*, as He shows us goodness and mercy while He willingly washes our feet. Hours later, we will fall asleep in the Garden of Gethsemane as Jesus sweats blood and agrees to carry out His Father's plan, establishing a New Covenant—offering Himself as the perfect sacrifice for our sins.

We will once again turn towards Calvary, towards the cross and contemplate our Savior silently suffering on our behalf. It is Friday. Jesus is on the cross. It is 3:00 p.m., and He cries out His last words and breathes His last breath. The sky is dark. The rocks split, and the curtain is torn.

At this point, for those present, Sunday's a long way off, and, worse than that, they don't have our perspective. Their friend is gone, they feel alone and helpless. Immense vulnerability is at the core of their immense grief. They wait. (We spoke about "waiting" last Advent; do you recall?) Consider how these men and women of the Bible must have waited.

As they wait, the sun sets and rises twice. Alas their Jesus, our Jesus, walks triumphantly out of the tomb meeting us outside and asks us– like He asks Mary: "Why are you crying?"

{Pause for a moment of silence.}

Our King has risen! He has risen indeed! He doesn't blame, and He doesn't hate, and He doesn't turn His back on us. Instead, He offers us His *shalom*. He offers us His love. It is ours for the taking. And all He wants us to do is love Him in return. Love Him for who He is, our Friend. He asks us also to love all those whom He loves.

He is the Alpha and the Omega, the First and the Last, the Beginning and the End. He is the new Adam and offers us far more than dust. "Christ has indeed been raised from the dead, the firstfruits of those who have fallen asleep. For since death came through a man, the Resurrection of the dead also comes through a man. For as in Adam all die, so in Christ all will be made alive. But each in his own turn: Christ, the firstfruits; then when he comes, those who belong to him." {Note to self: The Scripture reference here 1 Corinthians 15:20 –23.} "And just as we have borne the likeness of the earthly man, so shall we bear the likeness of the man from heaven" {49}.

Therefore, my dear brothers (and sisters!), stand firm! Let nothing move you because this is not only where we are headed, this is where we are.

Always give yourselves fully to the work of the Lord, because you know that "your labor in the Lord is not in vain" {58}.

Praise be to God! Alleluia! Amen.

{Ask congregation to quietly listen to song and exit the sanctuary in silence.}

* * *

The pianist got out of his seat and as quietly as he could, he made his way to the piano. The cantor did the same, making her way to the lectern. Together they filled the sanctuary with their beautiful rendition of "Were You There (When They Crucified My Lord)."

All the retreatants, and even Josh himself, were deeply touched by the reflections and the exquisite song. It is possible that Keith may have been the one who was most deeply moved by Josh's words as he recognized that they seemed to echo many of the same sentiments from the essay, which he had written all those years ago. This reminded him to ask his mother if she had found her copy of it.

A Spirituality of Waiting

During Sarah's prayer time the following day, she was led to contemplate "waiting" because it seemed to keep coming up almost as a theme. She considered how difficult it must have been for her husband to wait to tell her of Gloria's passing until they returned home. Although she had been unaware at the time, *he* knew that her world had been altered forever. Sarah recognized that for all those months down south he couldn't share his own grief with his best friend—his wife. She often thought about where Gloria is now. Sarah grappled with the juxtaposition that although Gloria's spirit is present with the Lord, her body is yet, simultaneously, *waiting* for the Resurrection.

Sarah surmised that her contemplations on "waiting" were initiated by the Advent Reflection she had been given by Deacon Josh who posed the question, "Regardless of the manner in which you wait, are you feeling God's love in that place?" And now, reflecting on last night's Lenten Retreat, she feels she is being invited more deeply into this contemplation. Sarah was most especially touched by the question Jesus posed to His disciples in the Garden of Gethsemane, "Could you not stay awake and pray with me?" She considered how exhausted the disciples must have been and was generously sympathetic towards their conduct because of the human condition of tiredness, which prevented them from waiting with Jesus in the way He needed.

All these thoughts led her to Galatians 5:22 and the fruit of the Spirit, "Love, joy, peace, *patience*, goodness, kindness, faithfulness, gentleness, and self-control," with patience being the one the Lord seemed to be highlighting. *Why is the Lord calling this to my attention*, she considered as she sat alone in the Florida Room deep in prayer.

She was sitting quietly in the silence, waiting for some type of clarity, when suddenly, yet gently, the answer seemed to come forth from deep within her spirit. It felt as if the Lord downloaded an understanding, which was far too wonderful for her to have developed on her own. "Ours is a Spirituality of Waiting," the Spirit seemed to be conveying and then a flood of examples ran through her thoughts. She hardly had time to consider the first example when the next one followed suit. It all happened so fast, she quickly grabbed her journal to write them down.

One after the other, the Biblical examples came to her mind in no particular order, and as she wrote each one, she realized that we are still being asked to wait, to be "patient," and to trust. Following are the exact words she penned in her journal, which represent many individuals, including Jesus himself, who waited:

1. "My hour has not yet come;"

2. Jesus waited in the Garden of Gethsemane (discernment);

3. Moses waited in the desert for forty years;

4. Esther waited for her moment before the king;

5. Simeon waited to die until he saw his Savior's face;

6. Elizabeth/Zechariah waited for a son;

7. Abraham/Sarah—for God's provision;

8. Hannah—for baby (Samuel);

9. Apostles—for Holy Spirit/God to release the Holy Spirit;

10. We wait for the second coming of Christ;

11. Mary waited for Jesus for four days after Lazarus died;

12. Woman with the issue of blood waited 12 years for her healing;

13. Israelites waited 200 years in Egypt to be delivered;

14. Joseph waited in the pit, then in the prison;

15. Daniel waited in the lion's den;

16. John the Baptist waited for God to show him the Messiah;

17. Jews waited for the birth of the Messiah (who came in the "fullness of time");

18. God waited for Jesus to take his last breath (3:00 p.m./ time of Passover);

19. Jesus waited three days for the Resurrection;

20. The three boys in the fiery furnace waited for their deliverance;

21. Jonah waited three days in the belly of the whale;

22. Israelites waited until they walked around Jericho (13 times) for walls to fall;

23. Job waited on God;

24. Jacob had to wait another seven years for Rachel;

25. Martyrs in the Book of Revelation told to wait a little while longer.

Sarah considered if she should dare write the last two examples because they startled her, but she did so, believing they would not have been given if it were not necessary: A certain someone waited for Eve to be alone, and he also waited for Jesus to be weakened in the desert.

Sarah was awestruck at the list she compiled in less than fifteen minutes, and she knew intuitively that it would take a very, very long time for her to pray with the list. She would wait patiently until further revelation was given. In the interim, she was again reminded of Deacon Josh's Advent Reflection. She grabbed her copy of it and reread the three questions he posed early on: "We can contemplate waiting in many different ways. For instance...Do you find yourself waiting *on* God, *for* God, or are you waiting *with* God?"

Her response, "Yes," seemed to answer all three questions at once, as she realized one could be waiting in all three manners, simultaneously. She waits on, for, and with God at all times.

Knowing she had much to ponder, she sat in the Florida Room while her thoughts took her back and forth between the Galatians Scripture and the Beatitudes. Pausing, she glanced out the window momentarily, and as she did, she suddenly became aware of the clock ticking gently in the room. It was a good hour before she was ready to conclude her time in prayer.

When she finally made her way to the den where Jack was sitting, Sarah couldn't help but giggle because his first words upon seeing her were, "Hi Sweetheart, I was waiting for you to finish. I just made you a cup of hot tea. It's on the mug warmer."

With a deeper appreciation for his patience, his bride replied, "Thank you, Dear. I love you so."

A Glorious Easter Morning

It is not easy to wake up before the crack of dawn, but each year Jack and Sarah commit to waking up very early to attend the Easter Sunrise Mass at the nearby Jesuit Retreat House. The happy couple used to attend the Triduum Retreat, which made it convenient to just wake up, get dressed, and go outside to the hill where Mass was celebrated. However, a few years back, they decided that they prefer to sleep in their own home. Foregoing the retreat means they have to set the alarm clock a few minutes earlier in order to participate; the short drive doesn't add too much time to their tradition.

The Petersons find the Easter Vigil Mass very dramatic, with the darkened church illuminated first by the bonfire then by the soft glow of candlelight, but they choose to attend the sunrise Mass when the weather cooperates. The natural progression of darkness yielding to the morning sunlight is a holy time.

As Sarah awoke from her sleep, the room still dark, the Scripture found in Isaiah 60:1 floated through her mind: "Arise, shine, for your light has come, and the glory of the LORD rises upon you." It seemed to motivate this tired, elderly woman to also coax her husband into waking up. "Sweetheart, it's Easter morning, time to get up."

Jack's sleepy response was in line with the circumstances, "Already?"

"Yes, Sweetheart. Happy Easter," Sarah whispered back as she wondered if it might be a better idea to let him sleep and attend a Mass later in the day. She couldn't help but remember how much easier this tradition was when they were younger and how with each passing year it seemed less agreeable with their age.

In the wee hours of each Easter morning, Sarah always finds herself remembering the little cat they had when they were first married. Jack had given the kitten to Sarah as an Easter present all those years ago; he "wrapped" the present by snuggling him in a blanket and placing him in an Easter basket. Sarah was elated when he presented the basket, from which emanated tiny cries of love.

The handsome tan and white cat, whose name was Muffin, was as sweet as his name implies. He was always with them as they awoke on Easter mornings, his purr filling the air with love. To this day, she still misses their little friend, and she continues to sense his sweetness and love, which are felt all these years later by those he left behind. His death was very difficult for Sarah, but she made her way through her grief and is now able to remember her beloved pet from a place of peace. Muffin had left an indelible mark on the souls of all those he loved, especially Sarah.

Unaware of Sarah's trip down memory lane, Jack muttered through his yawn, "I want to go, Sarah." As his mind became more alert, he started to recall how holy the Easter Mass is each year for the few brave souls who gather at the Retreat House to celebrate the Resurrection while watching the sun rise. Following that recollection, he kissed his bride then groggily got out of bed to get ready. "Happy Easter, Darling."

Tired as she was, Sarah followed suit as each were unable to resist the anticipation of the early morning Mass. Another Scripture seemed to accompany the lovebirds as they methodically put on the clothing, which they had laid out for themselves the night before: "Wake up, sleeper, rise from the dead, and Christ will shine on you" (Ephesians 5:14).

When they arrived at the Retreat House, they were a bit slow as they made their way towards their destination. In order to gain access to the path leading up the hill where Mass was going to be celebrated, Jack and Sarah needed to first enter the Retreat House itself. When Jack opened the large door, they were greeted by the overwhelming scent of the Easter flowers that had been placed in the rotunda. The scent was a combination of hyacinths, Easter lilies, and other botanicals normally associated with the holiday. The sweet scent triggered memories of Easters past while simultaneously welcoming them into the one that was just beginning. Their array of colors had yet to be discovered!

Once on the path up the hill, the moonlight helped illuminate their way. When they finally arrived at the outdoor sanctuary, dawn had not yet broken, yet they could see the retreatants had already gathered. The birds had also congregated, generously offering their sweet melody to the experience. All was peaceful as the Petersons took their seats. Jack turned to his bride and shared a random thought that had just come to him, which he prayed through when he had made the *Spiritual Exercises* of St. Ignatius many years ago. The line was as if Jesus had said to him, "If you do not follow Me into the joy of the Resurrection, how, then, can I share My exuberant happiness with you?"

There was still enough moonlight for Jack to see the beautiful, familiar face of his Beloved, and, through her smile, she joyfully replied, "I remember, Jack. I remember."

As Jack returned the smile, he kissed her. It was a beautiful moment in and of itself, but the moment was made even more touching because the retreat facilitator had just introduced music to gently break the silence. Softly playing, as Jack lovingly kissed his bride, were the opening musical notes of a very recognizable song. The tune of the deeply-moving Christian hymn evoked a sense of familiarity and peace.

The musical notes were followed by the song's glorious words, perfectly synchronized with the dawn's early light:

Morning has broken
like the first morning,
blackbird has spoken
like the first bird.

Praise for the singing!
Praise for the morning!
Praise for them, springing
Fresh from the Word!

Gathering the Graces

The Easter Celebration, and its message of hope, continued as the Peterson family, along with all Christians around the world, turned their attention to the feast of Pentecost. This festival is known to be the birth of the church. Pentecost, from the Greek, *Pentekostos*, means "fifty," and this year it seemed to take on a double meaning. With Easter Sunday now behind them, the Petersons, and all Catholics for that matter, began making their way through the liturgical calendar toward this special holiday. The Petersons, however, also turned their attention to the next milestone: Jack and Sarah's fiftieth wedding anniversary! Their Golden Anniversary was just two months away.

The first task was to prepare the guest list, and Monica offered to take on this responsibility. As she and Sarah sat down to begin the list, a tiny wave of sadness came over Sarah as it suddenly occurred to her that her lifelong friend, Gloria, would not be in attendance. When Sarah shared her disappointment with her daughter, Monica attempted to comfort her by saying, "Miss Gloria will be with us in spirit, Mom." Although this rang true to Sarah, she considered this a "both/and" situation as opposed to an "either/or" situation because both facts were true simultaneously. Yes, Gloria would be present in ways Sarah could not understand, and yes, Sarah was very saddened by her absence. Holding the tension between these two truths is difficult for anyone who has lost a loved one.

When Monica and Sarah completed the guest list, they

shared it with the others to be sure that no one was inadvertently omitted. Gloria's niece, Cassandra, was on the list, along with her husband, James, and their teenage boys, Joseph and Anthony. It was Keith who called to their attention that Gloria's brother-in-law, Bob, also needed to be added. Sarah was so grateful that Keith caught this because she didn't want to hurt anyone's feelings. She had once left someone off a guest list due to unusual circumstances, but in the end, this turned out to be the wrong decision. Jack also discovered that it is best to embrace the practice that "all are welcome at the table."

Lily asked if their two dogs and the cat could attend the party. Their grandfather gently explained that the catering hall wouldn't look too kindly on that.

Since Amy was the "family photographer," she was given the task of gathering pictures from her parents' lives in order to put a slideshow together. Amy felt slightly overwhelmed at first because the pictures came pouring in from the entire Peterson clan. She was given black and white photos from way back in the day. Also among the treasures were Polaroid pictures, which were all the rage in the seventies. At the time, the technology was amazing because the physical picture was printed in real time. Going through some of the older boxes, she discovered that most of the pictures were accompanied by the "negatives" that the developer always included, at no extra charge. In the now, digital age, these methods seemed archaic.

Where do I start? Amy thought as the boxes seemed to take over her dining room table. Her own thoughts seemed to reply, *At the beginning, of course.* With that, she found the nicest wedding portrait of her parents and from there decided to backtrack. She would begin the slideshow with pictures of Jack as a young child and make her way through his teenage years, college years, and the time he spent in the service. When introducing Sarah, she was able to begin in the cradle because her grandparents had given their daughter so many pictures of her as a baby and a toddler.

Eventually, the two lives converged; Amy found a picture of Jack and Sarah on their first date at the local soda shop. *Aw, how cute*, she thought as she looked at their young faces. She couldn't help but notice the resemblance between her young father and her son, Patrick. As she reflected on the resemblance, another similarity occurred to her. A memory of Keith planting sunflower seeds in the garden when he was fourteen years old flashed through her mind. *Wow! They both look like Keith when he was a teenager! Hmm, what do you know? My Patrick is made in the image of the gardener!*

Amy quickly realized that sorting through all the pictures put her in a very privileged position, and this thought transmuted her anxiety to a sense of calm. She had a front-row seat, witnessing their journey through the decades. Her study of Ignatian Spirituality informed her that it would be most appropriate for her to attempt to "gather the graces" of their lives as she understood them and portray them in the slideshow. The intangible graces were many, and she would attempt to capture them as best she was able. She recognized very quickly that she was standing on holy ground.

Amy thought that the best picture to follow their wedding portrait would be the one her paternal grandfather had taken of Jack and Sarah on the day they returned home from their honeymoon. Together, they were planting a dogwood tree in their backyard. This project was inspired by their wedding favor, which was a beautiful, tiny packet. The packet, which depicted a bride and her groom, resembled a matchbook. Although it opened as such, it did not contain matches. Rather, it contained a tree seed. Behind the picture, Amy found one of the wedding favors, which read, "Our Wedding Day; Jack & Sarah; June 12..." Time seemed to have smudged out the year, and all that was left of it were the first two digits, "19."

Although faded, Amy was able to read the back of the beautiful token:

> Thank You
> for sharing with us
> this special day of
> our new life together.
>
> Please plant these
> seeds to commemorate
> our new beginning.

Like her parents' marriage, the tree grew and eventually blossomed. It still remains a focal point in the garden behind their house, and many milestones prompted a trip to the garden to stand in front of the beautiful tree for pictures. As Amy considered this, it almost seemed to imply that the tree itself was a member of the family!

Amy continued to sort through the boxes for many weeks. She came across a picture of young Sarah holding a tan and white cat. Her mother was all dressed up and smiling from ear to ear as she held the adorable animal. The cat appeared to be enthralled by Sarah as he looked up at her. Amy recalled her mother having told her about a kitten Dad had given her when they were younger, and this must have been him. She turned the picture over to find her mother's lovely handwriting. "Muffin's 5th birthday/Easter Sunday." *Oh, how adorable*, Amy thought. *I'll be sure to include this one!*

And so it went that Amy continued to methodically sort through the pictures, collecting memories and gathering graces. The slideshow continued to lengthen with each passing day. She came across pictures of her grandparents, family picnics, and even ones of herself as a little girl. She came across pictures of the Morelli family and family vacations. One picture was of three young girls wearing aprons with sewing machines in the background. Amy surmised that the three girls were her mother, Miss Gloria, and Miss Gloria's sister, Laurel. The picture was most likely taken at a sewing class. Apparently, the aprons were the fruits of their labor.

Tucked inside the box of photos was a greeting card her father must have given to her mother before they were married because the envelope was addressed to "Miss Sarah O'Brien." She didn't think her parents would mind her reading it. Printed on the outside of the white card with its elaborate, fancy red lettering was, "For My Beautiful Fiancé." Printed on the inside of the card itself was, "I thank my God upon every remembrance of you—Philippians 1:3." Written in her father's handwriting were the following words: "My Dearest Sarah, I love you now, I'll love you then. I'll love you forever, the sweetest of friends. It won't be long now until our wedding day. All my love, Jacob."

Amy was deeply touched by her dad's creative expression of love. She found the gesture quite romantic. *A lost art?* she pondered. *I hope not.* As the project progressed, Jack's second daughter couldn't help but notice how much simpler the world seemed to have been when her parents were young. As the awareness of this simplicity came to her, so, too, did a desire to uncomplicate her life.

Amy was not surprised when she came across an extra copy of one of her favorite pictures of all time. Her face beamed when she saw it! She always refers to it as her "Deuteronomy 7:9 picture." Everyone knew she had named it so because they understood that she saw it through the eyes of her Biblical lens. The picture was taken on the day the twins were baptized. Weatherwise, it was a picture-perfect day. Everyone looked beautiful and happy in the portrait, including both of Sarah's parents, who were still alive at the time; each of her parents was holding one of the babies.

After the ceremony, Keith had suggested that they take a picture of the twins with their mom and dad, their grandparents, and their great grandparents in front of the statue on the great lawn of the church. Representative of its name, Holy Family Church had placed a poignant statue of Joseph, Mary, and Jesus in a small garden area. Joseph stood behind his wife with his hands placed gently on her shoulders. Mary stood holding the Incarnation in her arms.

For Amy, the scene not only represents the four obvious generations, it represents two others because her interpretation includes the generations of those represented by the sculpture. She flipped it over and found in her own writing the words of the Scripture she knew and loved. "Know therefore, that the LORD your God is God; he is the faithful God, keeping his covenant of love to a thousand generations of those who love him and keep his commandments." Her heart was warmed as she paused to reflect on the promise.

Of all the pictures Amy came across, the ones that seemed to affect her the most were of her younger sister, Jessica. There were several of her with the family on her third birthday. Another one was as sweet as sweet can be; it was of Dad and Jessica on a seemingly ordinary day, but there was nothing ordinary about it.

Jessica had been given a play tea set, and it was clear that she had invited her Daddy to a tea party. She had apparently invited her doll as well because it was seen slumped over in the chair next to Dad. Jessica was wearing an adorable dress covered by an apron, which seemed a bit too big for her. The curls of her hair landed sweetly on her shoulders. The necklace she wore was a gold cross, which was most likely given to her at her baptism; Amy knew this because, to this day, she still had the same one. Aunt Betty had given one to each of the Peterson babies at their baptism. As Amy studied the picture further, she suddenly recognized the apron as the one she had just seen a few pictures back!

The print showed Jessica pouring imaginary tea from her kettle into the play cup, which was set before Dad. Dad's hand resting on the table made the cup appear very tiny. The expression of adoration on her father's face as he gazed upon his daughter spoke volumes! *A picture truly does speak a thousand words*, Amy thought as she continued viewing the treasury of pictures taken in what seemed like a lifetime ago. She was careful not to let any of her fresh tears land on the prints. *She didn't live very long*, she thought, *but she lived loved*.

Including Jessica in the slideshow conjured up so many emotions in Amy, which she didn't realize she had held. Amy knew intuitively that she needed to take a break from reviewing the pictures because she had tapped into something very profound. She had always grieved for Jessica as a big sister, but now, a mother herself, she began to sense a touch of her mother's grief and how it might have affected her.

She paused to say a little prayer. Looking up to Heaven, Amy asked Jesus to give little Jessica a big hug for her, and she was confident He would do just that. In honor of her little sister, she went to the kitchen to pour herself a cup of hot tea.

Amy completed the project by sequencing the following pictures, according to the order in which the siblings were born:

- Monica, Jeremy, and Michael on St. Patrick's Day;
- Amy, Don, and the twins at the ballpark;
- Keith, Barbara, Rose, and Lily in their garden;
- Baby Jessica serving tea to Dad;
- The entire living Peterson clan—all thirteen of them;

Faith, Hope, and Charity were with them as well;

- A recent picture of her parents standing in front of their special tree in full bloom.

Once the slideshow was finalized, Amy asked her son, Patrick, to help her put it to music. The carefully-selected, coordinated songs brought the project to life. The touching slideshow was the gift Amy and her family offered to their patriarch and matriarch, Mr. and Mrs. Jacob Peterson.

The series of pictures highlighted them as a loving husband and wife, a very special Dad and Mom, and very beloved grandparents. The finished product was a testimony to their dedication and commitment to one another and to their family. Ultimately though, the story, which the pictures tell, testifies to her parents' patient, enduring love.

Jubilee

J ack and Sarah reaffirmed their marriage commitment to one another and, as they left the church, everyone looked forward to attending the much-anticipated party. Karen, the maître d, was the first to welcome Mr. and Mrs. Peterson to the banquet hall. Karen had taken an immediate liking to the Peterson family when they initially came to reserve the ballroom. "How was the ceremony, Mrs. Peterson?" she inquired. "I would have loved to have been there, but obviously, I had to work!"

"It was wonderful," Sarah replied. "Just wonderful! Thank you for asking, Karen. You are so thoughtful!"

"I love your corsage," Karen exclaimed.

"Thanks. It's lovely, isn't it? My son made it for me. He's a florist. He made wrist ones for all the girls, too!" Scanning the room, Karen spotted several of the women wearing the gorgeous wrist corsages. The ones she saw matched each of the women's dresses, and she thought to herself, *this family is amazing*!

She had hardly had the thought when a little girl came running up to one of the women yelling, "Mommy, this room is so beautiful! It's like a fairytale!" It was Lily. Her face was beaming, and as she raised her arm to hug her mother, Karen could see that she, too, had a tiny matching wrist corsage. Karen was in awe. In a matter of moments, she had seen four of the seven corsages Keith had made for all the women in the Peterson family. Only one man sported a boutonniere—his dad had a single, pale red carnation on his lapel.

Looking around the decorated ballroom, Sarah gasped at the incredible sight! Each table was lovingly adorned with a pink tablecloth laying on top of a larger white one. The silverware wasn't silver at all; rather, it was golden in color. The matching plates were white with gold trim—all carefully selected for the Golden Anniversary Celebration. The centerpieces on the tables were breathtaking—a true botanical delight! The scent of the vast array of colorful flowers smelled as sweet as they were beautiful. It was apparent that, yet again, her son had outdone himself in creating the gorgeous displays.

Although they were too small to see from across the room, a tiny surprise waited for each guest to discover, including Sarah herself. After having come across her parents' wedding favor, Amy showed it to Keith. Together, they had a similar party favor created, only this time, the little "matchbook" contained wildflower seeds as opposed to a black pine tree seed. The sentiment on each favor read, "Grow old along with me, the best is yet to be."

Both Amy and Keith were very pleased with the way the party favors turned out. Keith was especially impressed. He had taken a few home, and one morning during his prayer time, he held the seed packets in his hands. For a long while, he reflected on his understanding of seedtime and harvest, which he had learned not only from his earthly parents, but also from his Heavenly Father as well. As he quietly sat holding the wildflower seeds, he thought it best to involve young Rose and Lily with planting/cultivating them. In the coming days, he would ask the girls to help plant and water the seeds. It would be exciting to tend to the tiny shoots as they emerge from the soil. The experience would also allow him to introduce them to the laws of sowing and reaping, seedtime, and harvest.

This was truly a special day, and Sarah's face was as radiant as the exquisite crystal chandeliers hovering over the ballroom. She looked absolutely beautiful in her pink and white gown with its adorable bolero jacket. The upper portion of the gown was white with an intricate lace neckline; the pink jacket was adorned with shimmering, floral pink appliques. The skirt of the gown was also pink. Her jewelry accented her choice of colors, with all pieces being yellow gold since this was, after all, their Golden Jubilee. She even wore silver sandals with flecks of gold.

Her groom looked as handsome as ever in his pale pink jacket, white shirt, and rust-colored tie, which he wore, not because it was his first choice, but because it meant so much to his bride that they dress in similar colors. Besides, they both knew the pictures would be absolutely precious, and so they were.

Much like the room, the two elderly lovebirds were quite the sight to behold, and everyone who saw them smiled with delight. Jack and Sarah's relationship gave all the onlookers hope because their love and respect toward one another pointed to something greater—something each of us longs to discover. Through all the complexities of life, through all its ups and downs, Mr. and Mrs. Peterson had managed to not only find love, but they were able to discern how to maintain and cherish it. They love one another as they had promised—to have and to hold for better, for worse; for richer, for poorer; in sickness and in health, 'til death do them part.

They loved one another on their wedding day fifty years ago and when they planted the dogwood tree the day after their honeymoon. They loved one another at the birth of their four children, and they each served as a crutch to the other as they mourned, grieved, and buried one of them. They loved each other through good times and bad—through employment opportunities and through job losses. They laughed together, and they cried together. They went on vacations together, and they returned home. They helped one another at the grocery store, and they prayed together in church. They had arguments, and they reconciled. They didn't always get it right, but, by the grace of God, they were able to learn to forgive. Together, they lived through well over 18,250 sunrises and shared just as many sunsets, but they *never* let the sun go down on their anger.

What God had brought together, no force was able to disband because they lived in agreement with the Scripture that defined their union, Genesis 2:24. They also trusted, as they learned from Ecclesiastes, that a three-strand cord truly is "not quickly broken."

While the maître d had gotten the attention of Sarah, Jack's grandchildren had gotten his. They all ran up to hug him, and he was just as eager to embrace them. In this moment, it dawned on him that all these young children existed as a result of his and Sarah's love for one another. *Incredible*, he thought. After the last grandchild received her hug, he turned to reunite with Sarah. As he approached his lovely bride, he extended his right hand toward her and inquired, "May I have this dance?"

"You may," Sarah playfully replied, her face still beaming as she looked deeply into the eyes of the one who called her his Beloved. Sarah was just as happy as she was on the Sunday she had married him all those decades ago, and if it is at all possible, perhaps even more so!

Their dance began with a gentle kiss, and as the dance continued, each embracing the other as they had for the past fifty plus years, Jack happened to notice the slideshow playing on the screen towards the front of the ballroom. He gently pointed it out to Sarah to show her what he was seeing. As she turned to look, the crowds began to lovingly cheer.

One of the crowds gathered with them was the one in the banquet hall. The crowd completely surrounded them in a circle of love; the love was almost as tangible as it was visible. Present among the many guests were the entire Peterson clan, including Jack's sister, Betty. Fr. Dominick was also present. As he witnessed the beautiful expression of God's love dancing at the center of the ballroom, he was mentally rehearsing what he would say in his opening prayer. Jack and Sarah had asked him to do this once they were all seated. He wanted to remember to point out that the love of God was palpable in the room. Next to him stood Deacon Josh and his wife, Christine.

Cassandra and her family, including her father, Bob, were also at the gathering. Standing with Cassandra's sons, Anthony and Joseph, was their best friend, Philip. Philip's dad was beside him. Also in attendance were all the women from Sarah's Bible study group as well as some of Jack's former coworkers, whom he had known for a very long time. Many others were present who walk with them on this journey called life. Even their new-found friend, Karen, the maître d, was honored to be present among the many guests.

Sadly, there were two men who were not in attendance: Jack's brothers. Frank was absent because he had passed away a few years back. His estranged brother, Tom, was absent not because he had passed away, nor because he wasn't invited, but because his RSVP simply stated, "No." Despite Tom's absence, Jack was at peace because he knew in his heart that by extending an invitation to his estranged brother, he had held true to his belief that, "all are welcome to the table."

* * *

There was a second crowd of onlookers that was almost as visible as it was tangible. It consisted of all those who had gone on to Heaven before them. Its members were the cloud of witnesses spoken of in Hebrews 12, the communion of saints.

Each guest was all dressed up for the special occasion. They were seated at banquet tables themselves. Each table displayed its own unique floral arrangement, which had been created by the Divine Gardener Himself. The centerpieces contained numerous species of flowers in an array of glorious colors not found on this earth. The scent that seemed to be the most pungent was that of heavenly roses. The large, almost indescribable, gorgeous bouquets seemed to be emanating light.

Their "ballroom" was not a room at all. It was an expansive outdoor space with no walls. The weather was perfect as usual, and the guests were quite comfortable. A cool breeze gently danced around them. There wasn't a cloud in the sky except for the soft, fluffy white one that had been strategically placed overhead. The cumulus cloud served as a decorative canopy for those gathered on the veranda. Somehow, the angels had placed streams of pink flowers on it, which hung beautifully overhead. It was breathtaking!

A large assortment of birds had congregated and were sweetly singing in celebration of the festivities. Their songs harmoniously joined those of the angels, and the music was an auditory delight! It was another glorious "day" in Heaven by all accounts—another "day" in Paradise.

Present among these guests were Jack and Sarah's parents and grandparents, Jack's brother, Frank, as well as several of their aunts and uncles. Gloria Morelli and her family were also present, just as Monica had said she would be. Their precious daughter, Jessica, was also in attendance, sitting proudly as she watched her parents dancing with tears in their eyes and smiles on their faces. Although her parents had aged since she had closed her eyes on that crisp, cool day in October all those years ago, she still recognized them; she knew them through the powerful cord of love that forever bound them together. Jessica was beaming as she took it all in.

Jessica turned to her young friend, Melissa Johnson, who was seated at her table, and proudly informed her, "That's my Mommy and Daddy!" She had met Melissa shortly after arriving in Heaven, and they were instant friends. The two young girls were introduced to one another by Gloria Morelli. Gloria had known Melissa when they were little girls. In fact, shortly after Melissa had died, her dad, Mr. Johnson, gifted young Gloria with Melissa's bicycle. Once they were reunited, Gloria was quick to thank her for it.

Sitting on Jessica's lap was her mother's tan and white cat, Muffin, whom she was hugging very tenderly. In the split second when the thin veil between Heaven and earth had been temporarily parted, Muffin suddenly became very alert. His ears immediately straightened up and turned forward. He stood attentively on Jessica's lap to catch a better glimpse of Sarah! He began meowing excitedly because he couldn't contain his delight upon seeing her again. Muffin was mesmerized!

The Lord, who was sitting beside Jessica, reached out for her hand to hold it, and as He did, Muffin, in turn, nestled himself against His arm in an effort to thank Him for the tremendous gift he and the others had just received.

Unlike Muffin who was focused solely on Sarah, Jessica, who was always an inquisitive and astute child, began scanning the crowd on the other side of the veil. She enjoyed having a glimpse of her family, and she assumed that the access would only last a short while. As she lovingly looked at the faces of all those whom she had known, she suddenly seemed a bit unsure of something, which apparently was very important to her. Knowing He could help her sort through her concern, she turned to Jesus. In her childlike, eternal innocence, she asked what, to her, was an obvious, but important, question. "Jesus, why don't I see Uncle Tom?"

Grateful for her loving concern, He responded with love, "Because he did not accept the invitation to the party."

Knowing full well the dichotomy of outcomes in *The Parable of the Wedding Banquet* found in Matthew 22:1–14, Jessica inquired, "Will he accept *yours?*"

"I hope so, Sweetheart."

Continuing to probe further, she asked, "Would it be okay for me to save him a seat at the breakfast table?"

Moved by her endearing love and compassion, Jesus replied, "Yes, Jessica, you may save him a seat in the hopes he will say, 'yes,' but that choice is his, not mine. Jessica?"

"Yes, Lord."

"Thank you for your prayer. I'll be sure he becomes aware that he has already been invited to the Heavenly Banquet."

Jessica was consoled by her best friend's response, and a sense of peace replaced her concern. Just before turning her attention back to the ballroom on the other side of the veil, she thanked Jesus and told Him how much she loved Him. In response, He gently squeezed her hand, which He was still holding.

* * *

All who had come to today's banquet were deeply moved by the love encircling Jack and Sarah. The Love was the thread that bound them all together. In fact, the Love was so strong and so powerful, that, despite his absence, it also included Tom Peterson.

Meanwhile, right this very minute, Tom was only a few counties away mowing his lawn. He was experiencing a bit of a conundrum because he surprisingly found himself feeling left out, secretly wishing he could have been at the celebration. Just as he was becoming aware of his true desire, the two little boys who lived next door had come out of their house and were playing in the yard on the opposite side of the fence. At first, the siblings were playing together nicely, but then it appeared that things had gone awry. Although Tom couldn't hear their words over the noise of the lawnmower, it was quite obvious by their body language that they were bickering, again. *Can't those two ever get along?* Tom thought, as he rolled his eyes.

Hmmm.

Despite the remorse and discomfort Tom was feeling in this particular moment, his sense of regret and annoyance was actually a moment of grace because it is precisely what Jesus plans to use in honoring the promise that He had just made to Jessica. It was His desire that Tom's discomfort would move him from his insistence on nursing his grudge to seeing that he needs to reconcile with his brother.

* * *

At the precise moment Jesus had lovingly squeezed Jessica's hand, Keith simultaneously raised his. Extending his champagne glass towards the heavens, he offered a toast to his parents. Calling out for all to hear, he exclaimed, "Mom, Dad, here's to the next fifty years!"

Others quickly chimed in. Among the various responses were, *"Mazel tov!"* as well as, *"Salute!"* A distinguished gentleman from Jack's entourage cried out, "Cheers!" while simultaneously, one of the children was heard shouting, "Hooray!" The assortment of responses wove a beautiful tapestry of the many cultures and generations present in the ballroom.

The last and most distinct voice that everyone heard was that of Monica's husband, Jeremy, who, raising his glass, called out, *"L'chayim!"*

Understanding only by context, and unsure of its exact meaning, Gloria Morelli's eldest grandson, Joseph, leaned over to his younger brother, Anthony, whispering, "Do you know what that means?"

Anthony, who is just as much a wordsmith as his grandmother, knew the translation *immediately*. Raising his glass of sparkling cider, he confidently replied, "Yes. It means, 'To life!'"

Gloria was beaming after witnessing the exchange between her adopted grandsons. She, too, raised her glass in celebration of Eternal Life.

Both crowds erupted with joy and laughter as the sense of celebration continued to permeate the atmospheres. In full agreement with the well wishes of his family and friends, Jack whispered in the ear of his lovely bride the very same word that Jesus was heard whispering unto Himself, "Amen."

Epilogue, The Coordinates of Time, Treasure, and Truth

I visualize each of the beautiful moments you have witnessed in the lives of the community gathered (whether in the earthly ballroom or seated at the tables in the Heavenly Banquet) as individual intersection points placed on a graph. I envision the graph as "the Coordinates of Time, Treasure, and Truth."

When the thin veil separating Heaven and earth was momentarily pulled back, Gloria Morelli, and those with her, once again witnessed the effects of **time** on those they love, who had gathered in the ballroom. Outside of time themselves, they are no longer affected by its consequences. How this occurs is unexplainable. Their ability to see current events represents my interpretation of the Cloud of Witnesses who "cheer us on," referenced in Hebrews 12.

The special moments at the celebration, which each character witnessed and experienced, created wonderful memories. Each added these memories to their collection of **treasures,** both individually and as a cohesive community. The vantage point shared by Gloria and her friends was vastly different from the one shared by Jack, Sarah, and their guests. The lens through which they were given meaning was also worlds apart.

The person who united them all together was the One who had parted the veil—**Truth** Himself; Jesus says, "I am the way, *the truth*, and the life." Jessica recognized this, which is why, without hesitation, she turned to Him to inquire about the obvious absence of her uncle. As Gloria mentioned in my initial book, "I realized it would be many years later until I would figure out that it was Love itself that held all things together in perfect unity" (p. 17). God is love (1 John 4:16).

Kindly picture a graph where the horizontal (X) axis = Moments in Time and the vertical (Y) axis = Lasting Treasures. Any given intersection point/coordinate on the graph would represent the emotional value of a lasting treasure collected/experienced at a particular moment in one's life.

All intersection points on the graph, therefore, represent a series of coordinates. I envision the field, the entire chart, as representing only what is true; therefore, nothing false can intersect upon it. Only that which is true can be recorded. Ultimately, the plot reveals one's authentic life, one's truest self. Although the horizontal axis never ends; eventually, it stops measuring time because, without fail, it will slip into eternity for each person.

This explanation attempts to demonstrate how my analytical mind illustrates a graphic image of a lifetime. The authentic, true self exists beyond the grave and continues to carry, and create, moments that it treasures (see Matthew 6:20), all the while holding on to all that is true. This thought process was the inspiration for the book cover I created for *The Coordinates of Time, Treasure, and Truth*.

The Truth is so powerful that it eventually exposed Tom's self-deception for what it was—a lie, and that became the only thing true about it. Tom's belief that he had the right to hold onto a grudge was now, and only now, eligible for placement as a coordinate on the graph because a lie that has been exposed is no longer a lie. The lie transitioned into a truth: "The truth is, this is a lie. I do not have the right to hate my brother" (see 1 John 4:20).

Tom's recognition of his having felt left out of the party is what eventually led him to work through his upsettedness. The second motivation on his road towards healing occurred one Saturday evening in July while he was watching television. As Tom channel surfed, he happened to pass by a preacher who was saying, "Unforgiveness is the biggest block to inner healing. We must pray for the grace to cultivate forgiveness…" When he heard this, he parked on the station to listen. In the coming days, he could not get the inspiring words out of his head neither could he ignore them.

When he felt ready, he reached out to Jack, and they were finally able to reconcile. On an otherwise ordinary day the following September, a coordinate was placed on the graph of his life that indicated, "I love my brother, Jack." This was an extraordinary grace, at which the trajectory of Tom's life forever changed.

As Tom spent more time with Jack and his family, he was amazed how loving and cohesive *this* Peterson family was; the sibling rivalry among his own children was just as real as it was in his family of origin. Distant memories would come to mind the more Tom reflected upon the disparity. He remembered how, when they were young, he would "check out" at the slightest offense. Tom clearly remembers one particular time when he picked up his soccer ball in the middle of a game and carried it off the field declaring, "I'm going home!" Both teams were stunned as that was the end of the game and the fun. He literally, as the old adage goes, "took his ball and went home."

Through his newfound friendship with Jack, Tom healed. He learned healthy boundaries and discovered that it is okay to need time apart. Spending time apart is good, but carrying resentments is just as unnecessary as carrying away that soccer ball, with far worse consequences. Tom's transformation is evident to all his family and friends, and from this day forward, he always knows he is welcome and that there will always be a chair for him at the dining room table.

Each of the brothers continues making his way toward his rightful place at the table of God, only now, their families navigate this life together because the animosity dissipated and was replaced by familial love. The two Peterson families continue to make new memories, collect an abundance of heavenly treasures, and purposely seek to gather many graces. Together they share life and are often heard echoing Jeremy's words at family gatherings, *"L'chayim!"*

* * *

I hope you have been blessed by either of my labors of love. If so, I respectfully ask that you consider introducing my books to your family and friends. Your doing so will help others know that they, too, have been invited to the banquet!

Shalom!

Afterword

Harmony of God's Love
By Arlene DeMar

Listen to the music, do you hear My voice?
Listen to the melody, do you know you have a choice?
~ you have a choice…

In the rhythm can you hear it?
Do you hear the subtle tones?
Do they echo words of love to you?
Listen closely to the tones.
~ listen closely, listen closely…

Softly playing, gentle, soothing as the symphony unfolds,
Awesome beauty–just embrace it; I define it don't you know.
~ don't you know…

Listen to the Silence, to the space between the notes.
Can you hear eternity ~ listen very, very close.
~ listen close, listen close…

Listen to your heartbeat, to its rhythm, to its song.
I'm within you. Can you sense Me? I have been here all along.
~ I am with you…don't you know, don't you know…

Milton Keynes UK
Ingram Content Group UK Ltd.
UKHW021833031123
431812UK00014B/408